CONTRARY TO RUMOURS OF HER DEATH, HELEN VAUGHAN IS ALIVE AND WELL AND LIVING IN SHOREDITCH. HAVING LEARNED A FEW THINGS ABOUT PAINTING FROM AN OLD BOYFRIEND, SHE'S SET TO TAKE THE ART WORLD BY STORM WITH A SERIES OF EROTICALLY-CHARGED LAND-SCAPES THAT WILL SHOW EVERYONE WHAT REALLY LURKS BEYOND THE VANISHING POINT. SOME READERS MIGHT HAVE ALREADY MET HELEN IN ARTHUR MACHEN'S CLASSIC NOVELLA, "THE GREAT GOD PAN". NOW SHE GETS TO TELL HER SIDE OF THE STORY.

"AND HE BECAME
AN IVY VINE

"THAT ROUND
HER LIMBS
DID TWINE"

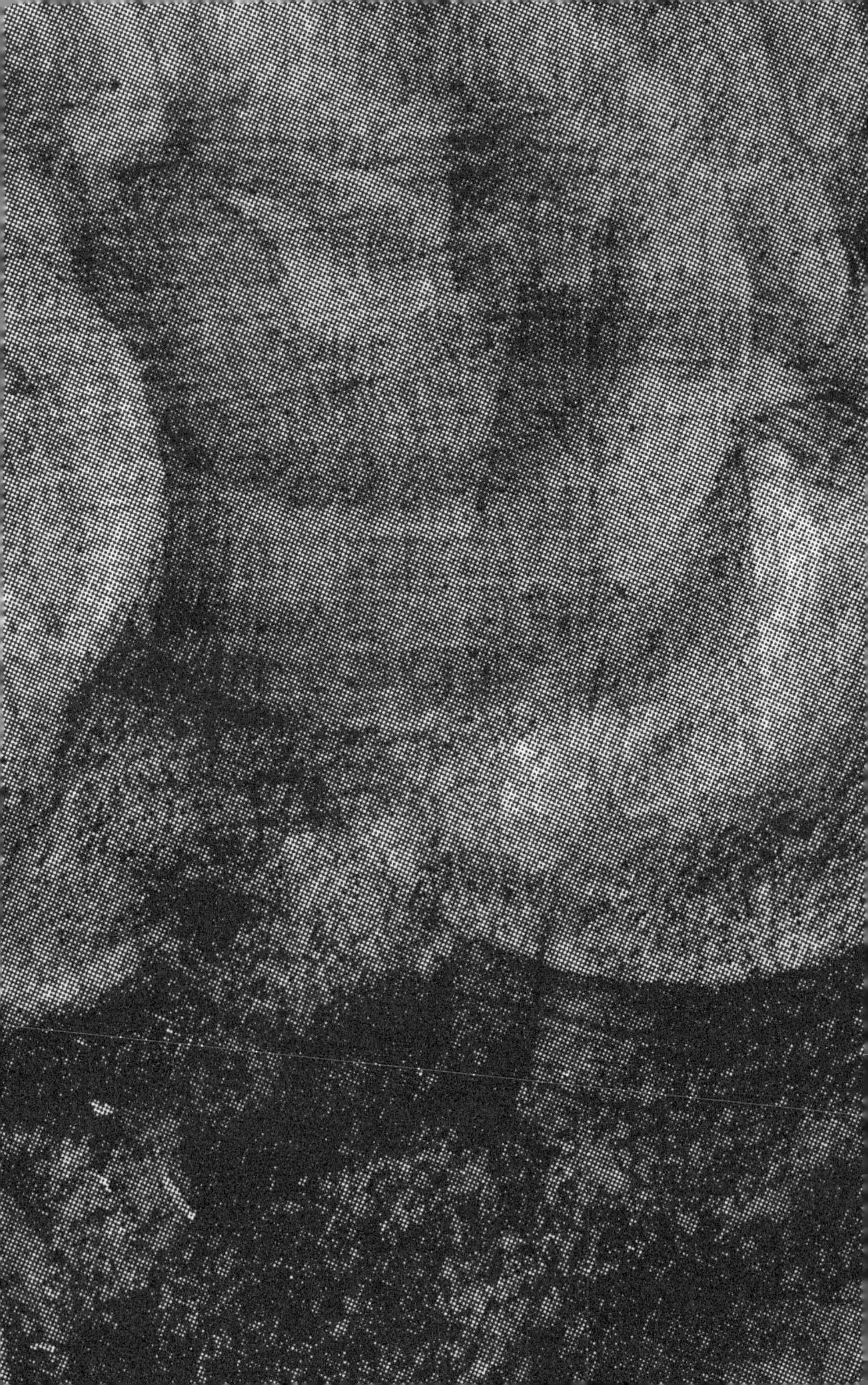

HELEN'S STORY

ROSANNE
RABINOWITZ

HELEN'S
STORY

2013

PS Publishing Ltd
Grosvenor House
1 New Road
Hornsea, HU18 1PG
England
E-mail: editor@pspublishing.co.uk
Visit our website at www.pspublishing.co.uk.

ROSANNE RABINOWITZ started writing when she helped produce zines in the 1990s such as *Feminaxe* and *Bad Attitude*. She laid out pages and contributed articles, reviews and interviews. Then she began to make stuff up. Her fiction has since found its way to places like *Midnight Street*, *Postscripts*, *The Third Alternative* and its successor *Black Static*. She also completed a creative writing MA at Sheffield Hallam University.

Other work in print includes stories and novellas in anthologies: *Never Again: Weird Fiction Against Racism and Fascism*, *Extended Play: the Elastic Book of Music*, *The Slow Mirror: New Fiction by Jewish Writers*, *Conflicts*, *The Horror Anthology of Horror Anthologies* and *The Monster Book for Girls*. She still writes a bit of non-fiction, usually in the form of extended rants on union, community and campaign websites.

Rosanne lives in South London where she engages in a variety of occupations including care work and freelance editing—plus the occasional occupation of the local town hall. She enjoys strong coffee, whisky and raucous music of all kinds. Though Rosanne previously played bass in a band called the Sluts from Outer Space, she now confines her musical activities to listening, dancing and writing stories about it. For more information visit: **rosannerabinowitz.wordpress.com**

ACKNOWLEDGEMENTS

I'D LIKE TO THANK members of T-Party Writers and Milford SF Writers who read and commented on *Helen's Story*, especially Gary Couzens, Denni Schnapp, Helen Callaghan, Al Robertson, Melanie Garrett, KD Grace and Jack Calverley. I also enjoyed illuminating discussions on gender, Machen and weird fiction with Allyson Bird, Joel Lane, and Gwilym Games from the Friends of Arthur Machen.

"The Two Magicians" (aka "Child Ballad 44") is a traditional song that comes in many versions, including a digital rendition called "The Two Webmasters". Musicians who've performed this song include the Empty Hats, Steeleye Span, Martin Carthy, Current 93 and Bellowhead. "Tom o' Bedlam" is also traditional.

And of course, this book wouldn't have been possible without the inspiration of Arthur Machen's writing. My take could well send Mr Machen on some rotations in his grave, but I like to think that at least a few chuckles will accompany the spinning. To find out more about him, visit the FoAM website: www.arthurmachen.org.uk.

1
VANISHING POINTS

"WHAT WAS IN YOUR DREAM, HELEN? You must tell me," demanded Dr Raymond.

"Leaves." I mumbled, the first thing that came to mind. But it wasn't from a dream at all. I was desperate to go back to sleep.

"Wake up!"

If I'd been a normal child I would have cried and protested at being disturbed. Instead, I sat up straight and gazed at the wall in front of me. As always, I focused on the large portrait of my mother, Mary, a dark-haired beauty who inspired reverential tones from the doctor. She is dead and now she lives in Heaven, Dr Raymond always told me.

"Helen? Look at me." Dr Raymond sat in the armchair by my bed, a notebook open across his knees and his pen poised. In the light from the candle on my bedside table his skin looked even more lined. I thought he was incredibly ancient, though he couldn't have been more than forty at the time.

"I wasn't going to sleep. I was looking at my mama."

Since I couldn't remember any dreams, I told him about my afternoon in the woods. "I fell into a big pile of leaves. There were so many of them it was like a bed. Then the leaves turned into little hands that tickled me."

"I see." Dr Raymond's pen moved over the paper.

"And then . . . my friend came to play with me. He was small this time, like me. And he rolled in the leaves and tickled me too."

"Did you like that?"

"Yes, I like being tickled. It makes me laugh." I looked again at my mother's portrait, wondering if she had ever laughed. Laughter was in short supply in Dr Raymond's house.

"So it was a good dream," Dr Raymond said, with a heartiness that rang false.

Dr Raymond was my mother's adoptive father. He always told me my mother was an orphan he found on the streets of London, who would have ended up in a workhouse or worse. She died shortly after I was born. He said little more than that. But from his air of disapproval I always assumed that her death had been my fault.

He said even less about my father, however much I pestered him. His most common response was: "I never met the fellow, and a good thing too." When I was older he went so far as to say my father could have been a labourer in the area for a harvest. But he, the good doctor, had let 'poor Mary' stay and I had been allowed to stay as well.

Dr Raymond saw that I had food and clothing. When he spoke to me, he usually asked questions: "What dreams did you have, Helen? If you do not tell me, I will send you away to people who won't look after you as well as I do."

Other attention came in the form of a weekly examination: he measured my height, the length of all my limbs. He listened to my heart, made me stick out my tongue. I thought this was to be expected because he was a doctor, though I'd been free of the usual childhood illnesses. But far from being pleased with my robust health, Dr Raymond often muttered as if that was another thing wrong with me.

In my earliest years he hired a wet nurse for me, but she didn't stay on. Another nurse, then a governess followed. They were sent away too. Whenever they began to care for me, off they went. But Dr Raymond himself would have flurries of fussing when he showered me with clothes and toys.

Once he brought a rocking horse from London. The wooden horse's lips were drawn back from the bit as if in pain, its eyes crossed and bewildered. At first I hesitated to sit on it in fear it would add to the creature's distress.

But I thanked him and smiled in the way little girls should when given gifts. It was a toy, after all. Don't parents give children toys when they are good? My last governess had read stories to me where that happened.

As I sat on the horse and rocked dutifully back and forth, Dr Raymond began stroking my hair. "I'm so sorry, Mary," he muttered.

"I'm Helen, Helen Vaughan. Mary is my mother and she is dead. Now she lives in Heaven," I informed him, though I was already having some doubts about where my mother might reside.

There had been an unfounded report of my own death many years ago. However, I continue to survive and thrive. I've gone by other names—Herbert, Raymond and Beaumont among them. Now there's no reason I can't call myself Helen Vaughan again. In fact, if you look up that name on Google, you will come across many of us. There's a chartered accountant, a maths teacher, a "regeneration officer", even a policewoman called Helen Vaughan.

And you may also come upon a few lines about me in a review of an exhibition at a bar at the eastern end of Old Street:

> "Among the repetitive installations and dour concepts, a most curious canvas by an unknown artist called Helen Vaughan

lights up a quarter of a wall. It is a feverishly intricate and fantastic woodland scene that's nothing less than Richard Dadd writ large. Watch out for this one."

This was penned by Naomi Harris, top art critic, maker and breaker of careers and reputations. There's a picture next to her review. Bobbed black hair cut in angles so sharp you could slice your finger on them; red-lipsticked mouth lifted in a half-smile.

"Richard Dadd writ large." I like that. But Naomi Harris was describing an earlier work. Now my paintings are getting much bigger, filling entire walls. I've gazed at *The Fairy Feller's Master Stroke* at the Tate Britain; examined the creatures watching the fairy axe-man as he prepares to split an acorn. The figures of the fairy-folk are meticulously drafted, yet distorted. I'm always drawn to the two women in ball gowns on the left of the painting. They have tiny ankles and delicate wings, yet massive calves, as if they've been working out on some magical gym machine. One of them wears a garment like a pointy-cupped Gaultier bustier, the sort of garment once popularised by Madonna.

While I appreciate the comparison, Dadd's painting is so small you need a magnifying glass to see its details. In the end, Dadd just didn't get it. If you really want to split that acorn, you have to think big.

I assume that Dadd did not work in the nude, as I do. The air currents brush my skin as I push paint around the canvas; they intensify my strokes. As I climb up and down the ladder, my legs tremble. My brush drips in my haste. Paint spatters my thighs, it turns to brilliant mud between my toes.

I'm relatively new to this, though I made my first efforts many years ago. An old boyfriend in Buenos Aires, an artist called Meyrick, first taught me the basics of perspective. I was fascinated by the concept of the vanishing point. As I remember Buenos Aires, I dash yellow and deep pink, viridian and purple on the painting.

"What happens when you walk as far as the vanishing point?" I once asked Meyrick. "Do you vanish too?"

I'd been taught the vanishing point lies on the horizon. Now I think it can be anywhere. Perhaps I'll find it in the heart of this glade. I rummage through a toolbox filled with treasured objects. I take out a long bronze and gold pinion feather; stroke my arm with it for a moment. I glance towards a trunk in the corner where I keep my other artefacts.

I settle on a pressed leaf with five fronds, like a thumb and four fingers, scarlet veins of sap branching through the crinkled surface. I place the leaf on the canvas, dab linseed oil and glaze to anchor it. But my glazing has given the leaf a lift. Instead of pointing towards the grove, it leads my eye to the section on the right. This is still virtually blank: a space of undefined green.

I make random dabs and jabs with my brush to suggest a meadow there. I add winter brown to the green, dotting in flowers of spring and summer, the rust reds of autumn . . . All seasons at once.

I empty my mind of everything but this fictitious field. I stare at it until the dabs of colour take on their own life, catching light to suggest colours I've never known. The colour-forms flow and coalesce. Are they flowers and plants, or something else?

And then I imagine a definite *someone* in this space.

It's Rachel, my friend Rachel, who was last seen walking in a field.

I sit down, and keep looking. I think about where Rachel could have gone, and what I can show of it.

13

The light in my studio starts to dim; shadows spread over the field. I look for traces of Rachel within those shadows.

Before I know it, hours have passed. *When you mature you'll lose the habit of measuring time,* my companion once told me. But I'm not entirely the same as him. I need to keep appointments. I must get ready to meet Rory at the Belfry to take my painting down from the exhibition.

In the shower I close my eyes. I let it bear me away to a reverie where I'm as fluid as the water running over me. I hear a missed melody of wind and reeds behind the spatter of the shower.

Is it my companion, appearing at last? Then I realise it's only my own humming.

I sigh as I dress, choosing close-fitting trousers and a billowing cotton shirt.

I used to pay much more attention to fashion. In that respect, he *was* right about losing track of time. Without me realising it my wardrobe belongs to another era. Now I prefer classic, ageless clothes. I don't even wear much make-up, just some lip gloss.

These days Shoreditch and Hoxton are no longer the dank districts I once knew. At night people drink and laugh outside pubs, and move in groups to the next club. Some say the area's ruined now: "The 'Ditch is dead!" So it may be. But if you go east, it's different. People come and go. It's a place where you can be anonymous *and* notorious. So I've settled into the top floor of a warehouse between Shoreditch and Bethnal Green, my living quarters and studio.

In the old days I loved my salons, the entertainments and explorations I hosted. But at the moment it's just me and my painting. Despite my history as a socialite, I'm no stranger to being alone. I grew used to it at an early age when I lived in Dr Raymond's house.

If he wasn't out seeing a patient, he'd shut himself in his laboratory or his library. His house was made of stone and it was always cold, even in the summer. Silence filled its rooms and corridors. If I dropped something or moved too quickly, it made a noise as loud and jarring as hunters' gunshots in the forest.

I only felt at ease in the meadows, along the banks of the river and in the forest. I would lie on the grass and look at the line of mountains in the west. I watched the mist cling to them and rise. I listened to the doves and the drowsy hum of insects and breathed in the sweet scent of the grass.

Now I live in a city, as I have done on and off for many years. In the past I dallied with the likes of Lord Argentine, Lord Swanleigh, Mr Collier-Stuart, Mr Herries, Mr Sidney Crashaw of Stoke House in Fulham. But I have also haunted the streets of Soho and Shoreditch in a poorer era. In Buenos Aires I sought relief from the well-heeled ex-pat milieu with forays into the barrios, shanties and rural abodes.

I have been accused of snobbery, but that's yet another lie.

Unlike the area's other watering holes, the Belfry Bar is full of ancient sofas, second-hand tat and frayed satin curtains. The walls are covered with graffiti and posters for gigs and political rallies.

I make my way downstairs to the rooms for exhibitions and gigs. Most of the work is still up. There's an edifice of twigs, severed stiletto heels, bubble wrap and a Wonderbra in a corner . . . *The Bubble Bursts*, by Hopi Harper. An installation involving Hoovers. A board of spiky cartoons; they're not bad. And an entire wall of photos from political demonstrations.

Then there's my painting. *Sprites*. Underwater weeds curl around each other like naked human bodies joined in ambiguous ways, white with a green sheen. A slender female figure lurks among the reeds and weeds. There are male and female figures around her, entwined in tangles of green hair, gleaming flesh, black eyes and eager, swollen mouths.

"Do you have a feeling this painting doesn't belong here?"

I turn to face the woman speaking to me. Her hair isn't quite as smooth and sharp as it is in the photo, and her lipstick must have departed with her last G & T. But it is undoubtedly Naomi Harris. She looks about thirty-five, the age I appear to be.

"I'm the one who painted it. And yes, my work is on a different wavelength, but this was my first opportunity to exhibit."

"So you're Helen Vaughan!" she exclaims in a throaty voice that makes me think she should be clothed in gold lamé and brandishing a cigarette at the end of a foot-long holder. "I'm Nao Harris." She extends her hand, but starts waving it in sweeping movements before I can shake it. "I love that painting and it was *such* a surprise. I often come here because it's just near my place, but it's really a dive. And most of the work is . . . who wants to look at *cartoons* and pictures of *demonstrations*? But your painting is an exception."

"Oh, thank . . . "

"I mean . . . " Nao takes a breath, narrows her delineated eyes and looks upwards, as she does when she appears on *Late Arts Review*. "The twisted lines lead you into a maelstrom of barely registered dreams and nightmares," she proclaims. "In the midst of muddy mundanity, this painting glows like a mysterious green emerald."

"Thank you," I murmur again as I begin to lift the painting off its hooks. "Say, would you mind helping me get this up the stairs?"

"Of course . . . How are you going to get it home?"

"I've arranged for someone to come around with a van. I don't live far from here myself. But size will be a definite challenge for exhibiting my other paintings. They just keep growing, they're murals really. It's fortunate I have such a big place."

I watch her register my "big place", along with my accent. Perhaps she has me down as a trustafarian, though the only trust I draw on now is the one I set up myself.

The painting is awkward rather than heavy, but our exertions distract Nao from pressing for more information. We go out and wait in front of the bar.

Rory drives up in a mud-spattered white van. He's got on the same Iggy & the Stooges T-shirt he wore when he helped me move a few months ago. His ginger-and-grey hair is still in a ponytail. But this time his glasses are held together at the corner with duct tape instead of Blu-tack.

I first found his details on the noticeboard in a local café. "Paintings will be pampered, no sculptures shattered", it promised.

He comes out of the van to help me put the painting into the back. He's a big guy in his late forties, not in bad shape. He certainly does handle my painting with reverence as he puts it inside, where everything is immaculate and upholstered in thick velvet. He drapes a loose piece of velvet over the painting and arranges it so nothing is exposed. A dust cover goes over the velvet.

Nao watches our manoeuvres with the same half-smile she wears in her photo. I give her a nod, then slide open the van door. Before I get in she wafts over. "Helen, before you go . . . here's my card. Maybe we can have a chat, or you could show me some more work."

"Of course. And here's mine . . ." I hand her a card I had printed recently.

"Helen Vaughan. Painter," she reads from it. "And this is your first exhibition? I'm sure I've heard that name before. Anyway, I'll be in touch."

As we pull away from the kerb I settle into my seat. "Rory, I have to thank you for suggesting I enter the exhibition. As you see, I've made a very useful contact."

"Yeah, Nao Harris. I've seen her on *Late Arts Review* when I've turned it on after the pub. She must've been slumming."

"Funny, she seems to think that *I'd* been slumming when I exhibited there."

"Yeah, well, when I first suggested you check out the Belfry, I wasn't entirely serious. I didn't think you'd really do it. Didn't think you were the type."

"And what type am I?"

"Fucked if I know." He says this with a smile. "I meet all sorts in this job, so I try to keep an open mind and I'm always happy to be proved wrong."

Rory helps me move the painting out of the van. The industrial lift comes clanking down and we're just able to fit it in.

When we enter my flat, Rory gives a nod of appreciation. "Your place looks a lot bigger than the first time I saw it, and it has fantastic light."

"It was still full of old junk. It makes a world of difference just clearing it out and putting in new windows. Let's just put the painting down there. I'll get your money."

I open my handbag, find my purse and count out his fee. When I look up, I see that he's staring at one of the new paintings. He steps back and tilts his head, taking it all in.

I wait. And Rory continues to gaze at the painting as if it's a crossword puzzle and he's just about to figure out a difficult clue. A curious reaction, not exactly what I'd hoped for.

"What do you think, Rory? I still have things to work out on that one . . . "

"It's very good, but I see what you mean. I'm a sculptor rather than a painter but . . . I'm wondering if you adjust the line of the horizon . . . And the grass, there's a quality that makes me think it's not *just* grass. Perhaps a few details can help there. And then that uhm, creature over there, move it around like so . . ."

For a moment I'm ready to snap at him to stick to removals and leave the painting to me. Then I remember Meyrick saying something similar many years ago.

So I thank Rory for the suggestion and show him out.

Immediately, I strip off and get to work again. Rory did pick up on something about the grass. Those blades of grass were little tongues against my skin as I stretched out on it. I haven't really shown that. And what about the angles and placement?

As I carry on, I see the range of this work take shape. Perhaps I should call the whole series *Helen's Story*, though I expect it to be a story about much more than me.

It's inspired by time I spent in Argentina, my earlier London life, areas of Wales where I grew up—the Usk valley, farmland villages and forests, the distant sea. But these places all meet at a certain point, and that's what I'm trying to show. That point—and how to get there.

These paintings will be too big for most galleries, so I'll have to bring an audience here. There must be an *atmosphere*. I'll invite more people to my salons, and not just the gentlefolk this time. There'll be more energy; this time the gatherings will work.

In order to summon *him* back, the unreliable bastard.

II
CARESS

IT WAS WHEN DR RAYMOND SACKED CERYS, a shy dark denizen of the Welsh valleys who became my best-loved governess, that my friend and companion entered my life. He was much more reliable in those days.

Cerys had come with references from a family in Cardiff, one of those who had built a great fortune from the trade in African slaves. I was sure she would hate it at our house after the luxuries and society of Cardiff, but she said she was glad not to be watching over five spoiled brats. Now she was able to play with *me*, a most interesting and talented little girl.

When we went walking, Cerys didn't fill the air with chatter, but listened to the breeze in the trees as if she expected it to speak. She even took me walking at night while Dr Raymond was in his study.

She told me that she had also lost her mother when she was a baby, so she knew what it was like and she'd try to be my friend. "Talking to the wind and the creatures in the forest is all very well, young Helen, but it's better if you're able to share such things. When I was a girl I listened to the wind and it told me I must be special when my name sounded so much like 'caress'."

"Helen isn't a special name."

"But maybe you have another one that the wind will tell you."

So I listened more to the wind, to the streams and fields of flowers that chimed with the night breezes and let loose their scents. Cerys told me about the earth children who played games in the woods when no one was looking, except for special people like us.

One morning, Cerys was gone. I felt her absence in the house before I came to a table with only one place set for breakfast. I ran down the corridor and hurled myself at the door to Dr Raymond's forbidden sanctuary—his laboratory and study. To my surprise, it wasn't locked. It opened and I tumbled into the room.

For all the fuss he made, it didn't look so special. Piles of books and papers stood on the floor and on the desk where Dr Raymond sat with his back to me. There was a bed, and sheets draped over irregular humps of equipment.

Dr Raymond turned around in his chair.

"What did you do to Cerys?" I shouted before he could scold me for my intrusion.

"I've heard the two of you mumbling nonsense to each other when you come in from your walks. Cerys was a bad influence on you, and you're bad enough already."

Bad enough. But what did I do wrong?

I burst into tears and ran from the house. I fled to the meadows and threw myself in the grass. I closed my eyes and imagined great vines coming out of the ground, wrapping me in their embrace. It would be wonderful to become part of the vine, and grow and bloom into flower or fruit. If only I could become a flower and turn a bright face to the sun. I'd rather be a flower than a mere girl living in a great draughty house with a grumpy old man.

Helen, you want to become a flower? You can become anything.

And then, as I lay in the embrace of the earth, I felt another being embrace me in turn.

The air touched me with more weight. The mingled scent of summer flowers swelled, taking on the scent of unknown spice, growth so luxuriant and ripe it verged on decay.

When I opened my eyes, I saw a boy who appeared a little older than me, but young enough to be a playmate. He smiled and held his hands out, waiting for me to clasp them. He wore no clothes, which seemed sensible in the hot sun. I gave him a long look and took off my own clothes. Dr Raymond would say that was wrong. But I didn't care. I wanted to be as free as my new friend.

"We are your companions," said the boy.

When he said 'we', he gestured towards the woods and the hills as if there were more like him hiding there.

His feet were muddy and pieces of leaves and moss stuck to him. He smelled of old leaves and new grass, like warm fur and cold spring water. There was a scent of sweat and the ripeness I'd smelled on the air.

He never said his name.

I had my own names for him. Hairy Boy, Dirty Boy or simply my friend. That was when he appeared as an ordinary boy. Other times he was much more. Then, it was impossible to *talk*. Could you speak to the sea or a storm whipping through the trees?

Sometimes I had to ask him to become a boy, just so I could speak to him. He would want me to bring a gift. It could be music, or a picture. I often brought him pictures of my mother.

He was happy to keep calling me 'Helen'. But when he uttered this ordinary name, his voice rose with an inflection that made it into another name entirely. *Helen, Helen.*

His voice was like the wind through tall grass. Or it was deep and rich like the best earth, like hot chocolate. Could this be what Cerys had been listening for?

I spoke to him about how I missed my mother, even though I never knew her. He told me he would try to help. He became a girl, a bigger girl with long dark hair in tight curls and small breasts with brown nipples. He urged me to drink milk from them. And then he took me to a forest, one I'd never seen before. I only remember walking a few steps, and it was so easy to get there.

He invited me to stroke the trees. I touched bark that was soft and supple like fine leather or a thick skin. It was warm, as if blood flowed beneath it. As I stroked, the tree grew breasts. But that milk was not as good as *his*.

In the woods near Dr Raymond's house we discovered mazes in the patterns of trees and caves hidden in the depths of the hills. I would chase him, he would chase me. Sometimes *they* chased me through the maze and caught me.

In autumn I fell into piles of leaves and rolled through the crisp and crackling upper layers. Beneath, there were faces hidden in the leaves, and the leaves were little hands.

I once described this to Dr Raymond as a dream, but I didn't tell him just how much they tickled. How deft they were and how they surrounded me, stroking and gently poking. I couldn't stop laughing and so many soft laughs answered me, coming from the centre of the pile, deep from a place where mushrooms grew and insects burrowed. I didn't tell him what it was like to roll in the grass, where each blade was a feather-light green tongue.

III
PIECES OF LIGHT

I'M WALKING INTO CENTRAL LONDON to meet Nao for dinner. She had arranged it at a private club frequented by well-known media people, performers and artists.

I take a turn here or there into an unexplored alley or hidden street. London is full of those, even now when so much of it has been torn down and built up again. Even now, when the ridiculous Gherkin rises behind me and the byways of an old island neighbourhood have been replaced by the sheer walls and blinking lights of the Canary Wharf towers.

Close to sunset, the golden cast of the air lights up streams of dust as they descend onto the pavement and touch the faces of people scurrying across it.

At my back is the braying laughter of stockbrokers at happy hours in the public houses and wine bars. Female office workers converge and giggle at another pub; I gather one of them is getting married.

Around another corner and I'm in a 1960s housing estate. Floor-to-ceiling windows and panels in weary pink and faded yellow reflect the setting sun; then I'm in the courtyard of an older redbrick housing estate with laundry-strewn balconies.

I take an alley that becomes a winding lane between boarded-up light industrial premises. There's a patch of green at the end of the lane that turns out to be a little park. I have found such unknown parks before in this odd area where the edges of the

City, Clerkenwell, Farringdon and Holborn converge. At the centre of this busy part of London I hear only the faintest sound of traffic, which seems to come from miles away. The gate complains as I wrench it open.

Someone has been mowing the grass and pruning the trees. But dust has settled on the rose petals, making them appear rusted. Much of the undergrowth has been left to run wild. There's a whisper of grass springing back into place after something has swept through it, a breeze like a breath just released.

Even in a big city, there are places that *he* favours.

At the centre of the park is a small fountain with a figure that might have been a young boy. His stone face is so worn that his features are a blank; the body is equally worn so he appears not to have genitals. Moss covers him. Water oozes out of a goblet in his hands, dropping down the sides into a trough around the fountain.

Bugs skim the water's surface, across my reflection. Beneath it stunted black fish laze about. I trail my hands in the tepid water and let my fingers move in familiar patterns. Again I remember reluctant lessons from the painter Meyrick. There are angles that lead the eye beyond what is known. There are angles and lines that point in a direction many fear to go. There are spirals leading to a hidden heart.

"You've been here," I say as circles widen under my fingers. "I know you've been here. Now you must come again. You know what will happen if I don't see you."

But maybe he doesn't.

I walk around the fountain in my own circles, then dip my fingers again in the water and anoint myself. "Come to me now. What will it take to bring you here?"

What will it take? I know of ways that worked in the past. Of the entertainments I arranged in my house, and the rites in the barrios. Other times I only needed to be there and I called without knowing it. When I was very young, I held his hand and walked into his world.

Looking into the fountain, I find a spot of light that is clear of the murk around it. "Pieces of light are found everywhere," he once said to me and Rachel. "You need to look through the pieces of light and find your way."

Has painting taught me how to look for those pieces? I concentrate on a spot of clear water that reflects nothing around it, a sliver of light that shines from another space. I touch the water and make it ripple outwards. The spot of light spreads and its touch against my flesh is like mingled cream and lemon zest. The sensation stirs memories of places I might have seen, of music I have yet to hear.

It brings me closer. Moves me sideways. Light turns solid; the solid things melt into light. The panes are boundaries between the now and then, the here and there.

As the planes of air and water shift, I hear *him*, my companion. Yes, he's been here. He's still here, making music as he moves along the planes, sending out waves of sweet shrill stuff that turns fluid, then solid.

Is he simply on the other side of this silent patch of green? No, he's at the centre of a grove never known in London. I only see his back. He doesn't turn, but lifts a hand to part the branches in front of him. The sun flickers through them, revealing lines of clouds, hills and haze, smudges of light and pigment that have no names in the world I know.

My companion takes a step through the parted branches, moving with a purpose he's not shown before. He's going, moving ahead. Looking past the vanishing point? *That* must be why I've not seen him for so long.

I stare through that prism of light and remember his words: *"I slip in, move between the panes. Think of the panes as membranes.*

26

Music and movement keep me free. If I get stuck between them they'll grind me. Or I'll be lost again . . . "

Careful now. Don't get stuck. I draw my breath in, ready to step into his world—even beyond.

But one membrane is quite hard when I bump into it.

I find myself sprawling in the fountain, the moss-encrusted boy impassive above me.

"Sorry I'm late, Nao." I brush the damp hair from my face. "I was working and lost track of the time. Apologies if I'm rather dishevelled. I didn't have time to freshen up."

My thoughts are still in that dusty little park, with my lurching movement away from it. The horizon flickering with colours I'd love to paint, and the back of my companion as he sets his sights on leaving. And I must go too if I don't want to be trapped.

After coming so close to his world, everything here jars me so much more. Treacle-coloured tans and identikit platinum locks adorn vaguely familiar celebs. At one table the raucous-voiced spawn of badly ageing rock 'n' rollers attempts to hold sway over the room. At another an American actress with the dramatic demeanour of a piece of wood is in close conversation with her ex. There's a young pop star whose lifeless warble pours out of too many radios.

"No worry," says Nao. "It's not as if I'd arranged a photo shoot. In fact, you look refreshingly casual."

This isn't an interview, it's only a "chat". But I'm sure Nao is sizing me up for future material. A new "discovery" would further boost her career or increase her collection. So, let her "discover" me. Nao would make a good publicist, better than any I could hire.

Nao regards me in a steady appraising way, and I return that appraisal.

"What do you think of critics?" Nao asks this suddenly.

I shrug. "I don't mind them. They have a job to do, and I'm happy for them to do it."

"That's a healthy attitude. People denigrate us. You know—critics are frustrated artists or a more erudite kind of groupie. But I never wanted to do art myself. Yet I *love* art. I appreciate it. I can write about what I see in a piece of art, and find effective words to describe it to others. I bring the piece alive to those who haven't witnessed it yet."

Nao stops her scrutinising and seems to look inward. I see the spark of enthusiasm, of delight in colour and form that once motivated her.

Then she's back to normal. "Unlike some critics, I don't write bad reviews just to show how clever I am. I concentrate on bringing work with merit to a wider audience. A lot of wonderful artists would still be toiling in obscurity otherwise."

I nod assent. "I enjoy good criticism," I say.

A waiter arrives. Nao orders a salad, but I go for a substantial wild mushroom and polenta starter and mains of roast ham shank and borlotti beans. Meanwhile, a bottle of Chardonnay arrives in a bucket of ice.

I attack my starter. The polenta is cake-like and crumbly; the creamy wild mushroom sauce is slick and pungent.

Nao picks at her salad and comments on the "gloriously unsettling" aspects of my painting. But she looks away from me—towards the corner of shrieking pop-star spawn—as if avoiding the sight of an embarrassing sexual act.

That only inspires me to tuck in more, while Nao takes a great interest in the Chardonnay. Finally, there's only a smear of cream left. I dip my finger into it and lick it off. The waiter takes away my gleaming plate, while Nao indicates that she'll be picking at that salad for some time.

With the starter gone, Nao is able to look me in the eye again.

"Helen, I realised where I've heard your name. A story called *The Great God Pan*. By Arthur Machen."

Just what I need. I clear my throat. "Nao, I wouldn't think that stuff's your cup of tea. It's not very . . . well, it's a bit old-fashioned, isn't it?"

"I read it a long time ago. When I was an undergraduate, I wrote an essay on Decadent art and fiction, which touched on that story. In fact, I'm surprised *you've* read it."

I stifle a sigh of weariness before I answer brightly. "Funnily enough, I do meet the odd horror geek who remarks on my name. So I read it out of curiosity."

"It's a peculiar story that somehow stayed with me. I think it's the way it evokes landscapes and moods that makes it haunting. Yet some of it's *so* silly, especially when Helen dies and turns into a pool of goo."

"That's not just goo, but an *unspeakable* mass that's neither man, woman nor beast."

Nao chuckles and pours more Chardonnay for us both.

"It *is* ridiculous!" I add. "Do you think a woman like Helen would be the slightest bit intimidated by some puffed-up pompous git demanding she hang herself with a 'thick hempen rope' or face the cops?"

I down my wine in a gulp. "And what real evidence did that clown Villiers have against her anyway? None. None at all. Those men—Lord whosits and whatsits—committed suicide. She didn't assault or interfere with anyone. I'm sure a woman in her position would have had a good lawyer sort out Mr Thick Hempen Rope."

I realise my voice is rising. I lower the volume, but soon I'm leaning forward and gripping my cutlery in what some may see as a threatening way. "What did Villiers say? Delving into 'Queer Street', was he? What a tosser!"

But Nao is not at all fazed by my display. She is really laughing now. "Indeed!" she declares. "But never mind about that. I'd like to learn more about the *real* Helen Vaughan."

29

Now it's my turn to chuckle. I shouldn't let those things upset me. And why should I worry? There are dozens of Helen Vaughans, and dozens of good lawyers if I find myself in a jam. But I *won't*. People are made of stronger stuff nowadays.

"How long have you been painting?" asks Nao. "Where did you study?"

"I'm mostly self-taught. A boyfriend showed me the basics and I just took it from there. I'm glad I took that path. If I'd gone to art school, they'd have had me producing a lot of conceptual dross."

"Do you think conceptual art has had its day?" Nao suggests, with a gleam in her eye that lets me know she would like the answer to be *yes*.

"Of course. Take all those Brit art offshoots—they only recycle the same clichés."

"So what do you enjoy?" Nao asks. "Who are your influences?"

"Well, you did notice the Dadd element. I'd also say a bit of Bosch, Dali and Escher. Perhaps a pinch of Francis Bacon, though he gets a bit miserable."

Then the main courses arrive. Nao is having another salad. I'm pleased to see that my ham shank takes up a platter half the size of the table. I start to rend the juicy flesh with glee.

Nao gives me a pained smile. "Watching how you enjoy your food . . . it reminds me of your painting. Beautiful, verging on the excessive . . . almost uncomfortable to watch."

"Well, there's more. I was thinking of holding an open house, a kind of working open house. You're welcome to come over for a look. Now, would you like a taste of this? I'm not one for starving in the garret. Or even starving myself in more salubrious settings, like the rest of these people here."

"No . . . thank you." Nao doesn't look away this time. Maybe she is a little tempted.

IV
ABALONE

THOUGH I ENJOYED THE FOOD, all that talk about Arthur Machen and the old days has stirred me up. I wanted to get back to filling that empty field, or returning to the grove where my companion parted the branches. Instead, I'm thinking about that fop Villiers as I slap on undercoat for a new section. He visited my salon once. It was also where I might have met Machen, who would have been quite young. Perhaps his friends brought him for a jest, urging a break from his writing and solitary walks. I recall several shy young men with a similar demeanour. Some of them stayed around, some didn't.

Usually, I told a retiring newcomer that it's fine to just come and talk. Or he could simply *watch* what happens upstairs if he is curious but unsure of himself.

Villiers visited my establishment once with Lord Swanleigh. Villiers had the florid lips and complexion of a man who grew up chasing an absurd object on the rugby ground and later drank much too much port. I understand that debating and rhetoric is part of the curriculum at the schools attended by people like him. It cultivates a love of their own voices.

He parked himself upon my divan and held forth on a variety of topics: the need to maintain order in India and restrict the entry of mongrel races to Britain, the writing of HG Wells, the idiocy of women's suffrage. He expounded and slurped his claret until the red of his face matched his lips.

Villiers also regarded himself an expert on the uncanny and more occult parts of London—or *Londinium*, as he insisted on calling the city. "Londinium is a very queer place, indeed. It was founded on human sacrifice by the Romans. Some may say that is why it's rotten to the core, but we're not only concerned with events in the distant past. Oh no, horrific scenes are still played out on the dirty streets of this city as well as the amphitheatres and vineyards of the ancient world."

"Amphitheatres?" I asked. "You won't find iron-thewed gladiators here. All that carry-on would wreck my china." I laughed, and my other guests joined me. But Villiers was not a man who would be taken lightly.

"How dare you!" He rose abruptly, knocking over his claret. Fortunately, it only stained his trousers and not my Nottingham-lace table cover. "See what happens to your precious china now!" With a swipe of his hand, he knocked over a sculpture of a male and a female Pan—or Panisca—celebrating a rite of love with a shepherd.

It was not china, but marble. It hit the floor with a great thunk, but it remained intact. In fact, it still occupies a corner table in my studio.

"This is an interesting piece. Is it very old?" Nao holds my little Pan sculpture and stares at the male god. Contrary to classical tradition he is rather well endowed.

"Oh no, it's only a copy. But I've had it since I was a girl, so I'm quite attached to it."

She gives a short snort of laughter. "And who would give this to a girl?"

"Another girl. A friend called Rachel."

Rachel. I've not yet added her to the painting.

Nao puts the statue down and walks about the studio with a click of stilettos, her khaki-coloured skirt swirling around her long, rather thin legs. "My goodness!" Nao is standing in front of the new painting, *Where the Places Meet.* "This one makes me almost dizzy! And . . ." A pink tinge leaches into the beige surface of her matte foundation.

She is visibly trying to control her breathing, making it slow and measured. I gather they learn that kind of thing in yoga and corporate stress-busting sessions.

"Do you like it?"

"Yes! Though 'like' isn't the word. What are those—"

The bell rings and Nao jumps.

As I expected, it's Rory.

"Hi Hel, the party started yet?"

Today he wears a Ramones T-shirt with a few reddish stains on it. Nao gives him a brief glance. "I remember you. You're the guy with the van. Here to move something?"

Rory scowls, lowering his gaze like a bull about to charge.

But he sits down and opens a beer with a flourish that projects the bottle top in Nao's direction. "Nah, I'm a guest at Helen's open house like you. I don't do removals all the time, though I have a nice niche moving artists. I know what they need, because I work in that area myself. This job sustains my sculpture, along with paying for my beer."

Nao nods, with a little smile that appears to be sympathetic. "I used to look at things that way when I was a student earning a few quid working in the Uni bar. Makes me a little nostalgic. But I'm glad I've moved on. Times have changed, haven't they? Past a certain age, if you haven't made it . . ." Nao shrugs and looks at me, as if expecting agreement.

Instead, I'm about to tell her that Rory had given me good advice about a painting. But Rory jumps in first. "What's so great about 'making it' if it means having to toady to a lot of twats?"

Nao raises her eyebrows in a movement that makes me think of a snake rearing up and hissing.

The bell rings again, quite appropriately. While I would have loved to watch the fight, I really must answer the door.

"Hello, is this the Helen Vaughan showing?" A hesitant voice comes through the static-laden intercom. "I mean, the works-in-progress? I got your flyer at the Belfry."

"Yes, I'm Helen Vaughan and yes, I'm holding an event." I buzz them up.

They enter the room like a couple of curious mice sniffing the scent of hidden cheese. The woman wears cut-off shorts and black leggings, her short spiky hair is the colour of caramel. "Hi," she says. "I'm Hopi Harper, and this is Alan." She points to her floppy-haired male companion. "I saw your painting at the Belfry, and I thought it was cool."

"Yes, I saw your work too." I'm puzzling over her name. Having spent time in the Americas, I know the Hopis are a native tribe said to use peyote.

"Come, Hopi, I'll show you around. Here . . . " I point to an improved version of *Sprites*. "This is the one that you saw at the Belfry. And this . . . " I point out *Where the Places Meet*. " . . . takes up similar themes, but on a bigger scale. Now, my two friends over there were having a most interesting discussion . . . I love reading about nineteenth-century salons where people had all kinds of lively debates. Don't you think that idea is overdue for revival?"

But there's no answer. The rather fragile young man stares at the painting, frowning. Hopi is eyeing the images on the canvas as if they're about to speak to her.

With one finger she traces the contours of my companion, following shades of ochre, white and brown and a touch of the clearest green. A hint of a grin that blooms from within; limbs that are slender but strong. Then her hand takes a different path, one that I recognise. I see the line of his arm, a fine movement of muscles under her fingertips as if he is reaching from the painting to embrace her.

Now she moves closer. She lets out an explosive sigh and leans until her whole body is resting against the canvas. She puts her palms flat against it. With her fingers splayed, she moves her hands over the scene. She reaches further, standing on her toes, then down again. Soon she is rubbing herself up and down against the canvas, breathing heavily.

Have I provoked this with my brush, the mixing of my paint? I'm lit up with the thought. For me, too, this is a pleasure like no other.

By now Nao and Rory have stopped their bickering. They are watching too.

"Excuse me, uh . . . Ms Vaughan?" Young Alan tugs at my sleeve and jolts me out of my reverie. "M-m-my friend doesn't seem to be herself. Could you . . . "

"Oh, I don't think it's anything to worry about. She's enjoying herself, don't you think?"

But he waits, shifting from foot to foot.

Surely he can speak to her himself. But I go over and put a hand on the girl's shoulder. "I'm *so* glad you like the painting." Her muscles jerk under my touch like the flesh of a horse twitching away flies.

She steps back. "I'm sorry. I don't know what came over me. I'll pay for the damage."

"No, no, you didn't damage a thing!" I try to reassure her. "I take your reaction as a compliment. Do you have any questions, Hopi?"

"Well . . . What's that . . . There are shapes, something happening and I'm just about to see it. And I *need* to see it, touch it too. It makes me remember, imagine things . . . all I've *wanted*. It reminds me of someone I *almost* knew." She is still unsteady, swaying then shifting her weight back as if resisting an impulse to press herself against the painting again. "It made me *feel* things. Sorry if I don't make any sense."

"We hold many shapes inside of us," I suggest. "What do you have in you? The images can act like a Rorschach ink blot. But I also want them to take the imagination to new places, help you see what you couldn't see before. So your response pleases me because it means I've started to do that. But the section isn't finished. And there's that big blank space over there." I stop for a moment, looking at the field where Rachel will walk. "Maybe you can suggest something."

"Is this, like, a mythical scene?" Alan is looking at *Sprites*.

"You can say that. But what are myths? They're symbols; symbols that stand for something that is often very real."

"Yeah, sure. Are these nymphs?" He points to the voracious and sly sprites, the couple at the centre of the group. I had shown them as very separate before. Now it's uncertain where one figure begins and the other ends when they're so hungry for each other.

Hopi gasps as if she is seeing one of the figures for the first time, a sprite with her legs spread. The sprite's exposed interior flesh glistens with green and silver mother-of-pearl iridescence, like the inner shell of abalone.

"Oh . . . It looks like it'll be all wet when I touch it," Hopi says.

"So why don't you?"

She unclasps her hands . . .

"No, not there!" Alan blocks her hand.

Hopi looks fit to slug her boyfriend. Whatever I'm trying to invoke, it's not a mere domestic spat, so I try to defuse the tension. "The problem with water sprites is that they're very pretty, but they don't have much to offer in the way of conversation." I shake my head. "You ever spend an afternoon with a few of them? It gets boring."

Hopi laughs, but Alan doesn't see much humour in my remark.

"We've seen enough. Come on, Hopi, I think we should go," he says.

"Yeah, okay. But maybe . . . "

"Give me your email address and I'll put it on my list," I urge them. "You're always welcome back. And, Hopi, you have nothing to apologise for. You've inspired me."

When the door closes Nao is pacing back and forth, her skirts whirling. "This is phenomenal!" Her face is also flushed; her fingers pick at her skirts as if itching to pull them up. "What I first saw was good, but this is exceptional. To think a work can be so powerful."

Rory pats me on the arm. "Helen, I don't know if *good* is the word. But it is . . . "

Under his hand the surface of my skin tingles. I feel a familiar sensation, a pleasant slither as if a fine-spun scarf is floating against it. My skin turns silken in response; my cells move and change in a new pattern.

For a moment I'm speechless with surprise.

37

V
DANCING BOY

I'VE SOUGHT THAT SILKEN SENSATION many times, and travelled far for it. The sensation used to be familiar, but I was young enough to take it for granted. Now I know just how much I need that contact.

I first became aware of it the day my companion became my Dancing Boy. My hands were sticky with juice from the blackberries I had picked earlier. But he didn't mind. His hands were warm around mine. The stickiness had melted into something clear and lovely. There was a prickling in my skin where it touched his. It was quite delicious. We were spinning.

He only held on tighter. We became one skin in our spin, and the prickling grew and spread the faster we went.

Let go!

I tumbled onto the soft grass, which was ready to receive me.

For a moment, I lay on the ground with my eyes closed. When I got up and opened them, I saw Dr Raymond at the edge of the woods. He was staring at me, and at my friend.

Then he turned around and went walking back towards the house.

Later, our cook set out my evening meal in the dining hall. I was between governesses, so I ate alone. I pushed my food around my plate and lined up the mashed potato, meat and vegetables.

I offered a handful of blackberries to the cook after she served the food, but when Dr Raymond appeared, I put my sticky hands under the table. What would he do? Send me away as he threatened?

"Please set a place for me. I won't be eating in my study tonight."

The cook set an identical meal in front of him—lamb chops, mash and sprouts.

"I thought I'd eat with you tonight, Helen. You must get lonely here on your own. I'm sorry if I've been neglecting you."

"No, I'm well." I put my sprouts in a circle around the chop while Dr Raymond watched. I speared a sprout with my fork and put it in my mouth. A high-pitched sound rang in my head, as if the sprout had screamed. Of course, it couldn't scream. It had already been boiled. But I *had* heard the grass crying when the gardener cut it.

"Who were you were playing with, Helen? One of the local children?"

I watched Dr Raymond's hands tremble as he cut his meat.

"Yes, one of the local children."

"I'm glad to see you have a playmate, but . . . it's better if you keep your clothes on, especially when the weather starts getting cold. I don't want you taken with influenza, do I? And it isn't right. What would your mother think if she could see you like that?"

"Dr Raymond saw you," I said to my companion.

That day he was the girl with long dark curls and small breasts. I still called him "he", whatever shape he took. I preferred to play with a boy because I didn't know any boys or men except for Dr Raymond.

39

Though he was only a little bigger than me, he did insist on growing the breasts.

Now he held his breast in his hand and offered. "Helen, please have some." I was tempted, but I was also determined not to be a seen as a baby. And suckling anyone's breast was certainly a baby-ish thing to do. "Don't you care that Dr Raymond saw you?"

"He has seen me many times, but he didn't realise it was me. Not then."

"Isn't this a secret?"

"It is, and it isn't. Everything is there for anyone to see, but they have to know how to look. And sometimes, they aren't looking but the truth will find them. Sometimes they will know it's there and refuse to admit it, but it makes itself known and they run in terror."

"You were never scary to me."

"Helen, you are different. You will learn later just how different you are."

That day he had his pipes with him and began to play, shaking his long curls as he danced in the clearing. The first notes were high and reedy. Then a lower register, powerful as my pulse in my ears at night. His fingers flew over his seven pipes. Maybe he had more than two hands for a while.

He paused on some notes so he could stroke his breasts, and between his legs. Then he started changing. Though his body was solid, it flowed as if something other than flesh and bone composed it. He kept the breasts, while his hips and legs changed and he grew a penis again. When his legs started to get crooked I cried out: "No, don't be hairy today! You smell when you're hairy!"

"You smell too. Everything has a smell," he laughed. "But I'll do what pleases you. I'll be what you want, as long as you dance with me."

Once the music started I was moving my feet in its path. He led me in circles, and circles within circles. He urged me into the patterns that appear under my eyelids when I am close to sleep. In the ground beneath my feet I felt the stirrings of the grass and the insects that lived and died within it, the rabbits and moles in their burrows. Even the stones of the earth itself came alive and boomed in cold voices.

I was breathing fast. The last of the leaves on the trees rustled in time to my breath. I lifted my hands into the air and whirled around faster. The dancing was not complete. Something more had to happen. Perhaps I will change too, and what will I be? If I spin even faster, I will soar! If I find the right pattern, I will learn his secret.

The music grew dreamy without losing its speed. With each turn he made, there were other changes. Hair grew on his lower body, despite his promise to me. But it was light and silky and didn't look so bad.

When I closed my eyes, the patterns behind my lids led me as surely as my companion did. I was learning, finding my way into the most secret pattern of all.

I opened my eyes and there—as before—stood Dr Raymond. This time he was close enough to see everything. His eyes were not so much on me, but on the pert breasts and erect little penis of my companion.

Dr Raymond's mouth was open, as if the sight of my friend stole the breath out of him. He clutched at his chest. I thought he might fall. Then he composed himself. Through teeth gritted with effort, he told me that later he would speak to me about *this*.

When I stopped dancing, my companion looked in Dr Raymond's direction and grinned. Then he grew. His hips widened and his breasts grew pendulous. When he became as tall as Dr

41

Raymond, his penis jutted further. Vines sprouted around his head and he grinned, his long red tongue snaking out of his mouth. It made me laugh.

I loved my companion, even more than I once loved Cerys. He was mother, father and friend to me. I stuck my own tongue out at the doctor's departing back.

The next morning Dr Raymond woke me and ordered me to dress for travelling. "You won't be going into the woods today. You will be sent far away from that creature, and far away from me. You will live with other children and be given an education."

I mount the steps to Rory's home, knock and wait. Nao has called him a "loser", and that he may be. But I cannot put aside my growing suspicion that he may be *my* loser.

Rory lives in a leafy area on the edge of Highgate, though it's not far from the "Suicide Bridge" over the four lanes of Archway Road. I remember this as one of the more miserable districts of London.

But Rory's steep little cul-de-sac is lined with three- and four-storey Victorian houses. Rory lives in a ground floor flat at the end. The front garden is full of elderflowers and long grass, which I prefer to the tightly trimmed gardens of the houses next to it.

"Helen! What are you doing here?" Rory is in dusty work clothes and he wields a blowtorch in one hand. "But come in . . . I was just about to stop work and have drink." We sit down in the kitchen, which boasts a bay window looking into the well-lit garden. There are twisted metal hulks and hybrid machines scattered within the tangles of vines and shrubs. Lavender explodes from the empty eye of an old TV.

The sash windows framing this sight are wide and high and would shout "original feature" to certain buyers. The windows are old and the wood frames have shrunk back to show cracks between them and the glass, but there are signs of recent repairs and painting.

One wall shows younger versions of Rory. Rory next to a vehicle configured to grin with big teeth, Rory next to the shell of a bus melted into waves with windows turned to eyes, cars arranged in a formation resembling Stonehenge. Another wall is covered with framed posters from old gigs and raves. Taking pride of place is a large photo of a smiling woman with dyed black hair, her arm around a young boy.

"Do you live here with other people?" I'd been assuming that Rory lived alone.

"No, but my ex and her son used to live here." He points to the picture. "We're on good terms now. I'm rather fond of the boy, and he stays over a couple of days a week. A lovely kid, though he gets into his share of mischief. You'd think that having him would be enough for her."

"She wanted more children, you mean?"

"Yes," Rory sighs. "And I couldn't give her much help with that."

There's obviously a sore point here. Could he be sterile? I am.

I look out the bay window again. "It's a nice flat. Do you rent or own it?"

Rory beams with pride. "Of course I rent it. It's a council flat! Bet you didn't think there were any council flats in Highgate. And it's a street property! They've been trying to get me out for years by not doing repairs so they can sell the flat off to yuppies. This is the only council house left on this street. An old lady lives upstairs, and they're doing their best to hasten her death. But neither of us are budging!" He takes a beer out of the fridge and passes another to me. "Our tenancy started before laws that made it easy to raise rents came in, so it's low even for a council flat... especially one in Highgate!"

I nod my appreciation. "But what does your old lady upstairs think about your stuff in the garden? And messing about with a blowtorch?"

"She doesn't mind, especially when I made her some window boxes. Fancy a look outside?"

As I walk out the garden door, the first thing I notice is the tree near it. The bark has been polished and leather stretched over it, and in the knots and hollows of the tree there is fur.

I run my hand over a knot of wood, and stroke the stiff pink fun fur. "Where'd you get the idea for this? It's great." I know he didn't get it from me, because I haven't painted *those* trees yet.

"Oh, I've been doing them for this guy who's opening a club. I just thought of it when he said he wanted 'weird trees'. I don't know. Or maybe I drew a picture of something like this when I was a kid."

"Is that what you got up to when you were a kid? Are from you around here?"

"Probably. But I don't know exactly where or when I was born. I was adopted."

"So was I. Or rather, my mother was. She was very young when she had me, and her adoptive father kept me on after she died. But how was it for you? Did you ever feel like you were different from everyone else? Did you have a 'pretend' play-mate when you were little?"

He frowns. "No . . . I shared a room with two brothers, so I was pleased to get any time alone—last thing I'd do is make up someone else to disturb me. My parents told me I was adopted when I was very young. I also knew other kids who were adopted. We decided it was cool. And I hung out with a group of kids who liked art, electronics, nerdy things. I had lots of encouragement from my folks. So even if I was kind of odd, I had an OK time of it."

I feel a twinge of something. Could it be envy? Whatever it is, it's best ignored.

"Show me more," I urge Rory. "What were you doing with that blowtorch?"

He takes me to the remains of a car. The metal twists around its seat, cupping it like a crumpled hard-edged hand. "Sit down, make yourself comfortable," he urges.

It's cosier than it looks, for he'd put more padding on the seat and within the shell of metal. This is all in luxurious purple velvet, like the cushions in his van. There's room for two people to fit snugly.

"I'll get vines to grow around it," says Rory. "The cushions get damp if it rains. But I found washable velvet so I can take the whole lot out when I want to clean it . . . "

"I can't hear you properly when I'm sitting in here and you're there." I reach out a hand and pull him in beside me.

And when I'm gripping his hand, I feel it again, the unmistakeable tingle of like calling to like, the crawl of cells unfurling and opening to embrace other cells.

"Helen, what hand cream are you using? This feeling I have . . . It's like the time I slapped on my girlfriend's skin cream after using a heavy hand cleaner. Then my hands got all hot and tingling . . . I really thought it was some nasty neurological thing. Then she said: 'Rory, you dork, you were using my anti-cellulite cream on your hands!'"

"Anti-cellulite?" I'm blank at first.

"Yeah, it gets the circulation going. So it made my hands tingle."

I slide my hand up his arm. "Feel that. It's nothing to do with any cream. It's a special current between you and me. I won't try to explain now. Just feel it."

But he gently pulls away. "Helen, I think you're an attractive woman and I admire your work. But maybe we should keep our relationship a professional one."

I'm not used to being turned down. If it had ever happened, I don't remember it.

Meyrick once drew a picture of me when I was in a rage. It showed a Gorgon with contorted, glowering features. I turn my head so Rory doesn't see that. I breathe deeply, and push it down where it won't be noticed.

"I really like you, Helen. But I fancy a woman who's more . . . shall we say, *robust*. Someone who's dead down-to-earth, likes a pint and a laugh and swears like a sailor."

The picture Rory paints of his ideal woman drives the gathering storm away because I just can't stop laughing.

"What's so funny?"

"Oh, I guess that's not me! Never mind, Rory. We can be friends." *For now*.

And just what does that mean? I've certainly had one—perhaps even two—friends in my long life. But friendship wasn't what I encountered when I first left the house of Dr Raymond.

VI
THE MAN IN THE WOODS

I WAS SITTING UP IN BED. Where was the portrait of my mother, the rocking horse with its pained snarl, the book filled with leaves I'd collected on my walks . . . all the familiar objects in my room?

I wasn't alone. There were rows of beds on each side of the room under an arched ceiling. In each bed was a girl, staring at me with frightened eyes.

One girl stood beside my bed, her look bolder. She must have prodded me awake. Will she ask questions about my dreams too? She didn't have a notebook. But she stood with her arms crossed, glaring like Dr Raymond when he saw me with my companion. The girl in the bed across from me held her blankets up in front of her, like a shield. Another girl looked like she was about to get sick.

I'd only been sleeping. I'd looked forward to meeting other children, but they obviously didn't enjoy meeting me.

"What's wrong?" But I sounded weak, as if I was afraid of them, and sad they didn't like me. So when no one answered I raised my voice to assume the commanding tones I'd often heard from Dr Raymond. "What is your problem? All of you!"

The girls shrank back and pulled their blankets tighter. Even the girl who woke me up scurried back into her bed. Finally, one piped up: "You were saying *horrible* things! You were talking about grass screaming when it's cut and a boy with bosoms and . . . "

That was my first night at boarding school. It would also be the first in a succession of schools where I would be accused of saying or doing "*horrible*" things.

Please come to me, I entreated my companion. You can be as hairy as you like. It doesn't matter what the others think, as long as I have you.

I spent hours flexing my fingers, testing the hardness of the bones in my hands, my arms, my legs. *You will find out how different you are.* But my flesh was solid and lump-like, no different from Dr Raymond or the other girls. I tried whirling in circles, hoping it would make me more like the companion who came and went as he pleased.

With each turn, perhaps I'll grow another year. Perhaps I'll grow up.

But when I didn't expect it, he was there . . . at the edge of a playing field where I was meant to fetch a ball for some game. I forgot about the ball and the game, and followed his beckoning finger into the woods.

In a lesson I looked out the window and he was there too. He was a bird pecking at the glass, a shred of night music that made the other girls cry out in their sleep.

I brought him presents, as before. I could not offer pictures of my mother, but I found or created other gifts. Pale handfuls of a girl's hair that I'd cut off in the night. A frenzied dance in a circle to my clapping that left five girls dizzy and nauseous.

A lace and silk bodice worn secretly by the stern games mistress.

Once I actually brought a girl, who screamed before he even appeared. She sobbed "He's here! He's here!"

"No he's not. And this is a secret," I told her as I grabbed her wrist and held it tight enough to make a red mark appear. "If you tell anyone, he will really come for you."

Soon I was expelled. I think it was for stealing.

After some years of this, Dr Raymond stopped sending me to schools.

When I was 12, he advertised in a few papers, offering a subsidy to any family willing to look after me. A farmer called Ross, whose one child had left home, took up the offer. The farmer and his wife lived in a village on the Welsh borders, sheltered by a forest and close to the sea. After the problems I had presented at the boarding schools, Dr Raymond told the farmer I didn't need lessons and should be left to my own devices. So I looked after myself, and the Rosses received Dr Raymond's money.

I believed my companion would find me as long as there were woods. I'd feel a hum between my ears, a delightful prickling over my skin. Music rumbled beneath the thickening air. He didn't need to play his pipes for me to want to dance.

As Ross had promised Dr Raymond, I was free to ramble in the forest. I encouraged others to come on my walks. The younger children loved them. We danced in circles until we fell, we found those hidden mazes. In the winter, I spent most of my time in my room. And though the elements made some games impractical, a foray into the snow still had its rewards.

He showed me transience, how rigid forms could furl and unfurl, expand and contract, move and merge. He showed me life and movement in still, solid things that began to touch and pluck with greedy fingers and sing in voices that set the trees and grass trembling. The scents released by flowers or the pines struck notes too, melodies that crept into my veins and pulled and pulled.

As I grew older, he began to appear as a young man rather than a boy. We returned to the forest where trees grew skin, far from the dead wood of dormitories and libraries. Sap, even blood, hummed beneath the bark. I put my hand into hollows where I found fur, soft and dark like sable, covering a heart that pulsed under my fingers. It was a pulse I recognised when I touched myself between my legs.

We sought out flowers with succulent petals that opened to reveal layer upon layer: frilled pink petals with scarlet veins, blood-red velvet petals shot with purple. The pollen from these flowers made me as dizzy as our circle games.

My breasts grew round and my hips widened; like my companion I became fuzzed with hair in hidden places. These changes came upon other girls too, but I was sure they meant something different for me. I was changing. I could change at last. I was growing up to become like *him*.

The licking of the grass on my skin grew more insistent.

He took me to a pond close to home. He played his pipes first, and the water moved and bubbled. It did not seem deep until we ducked into it.

Water takes many forms, like anything else. Now you will meet some of them.

The water flowed and rippled. Something gathered within it. A young man with coal-black eyes and long hair that was pitch-green, a green made of black. He was slender and long, skin pearly-white with the barest hint of green. First he looked around in bewilderment. Then he took in everything with an avid stare. I was equally avid for this new wonder.

Newly born from the water, the way you were born from a woman.

I had to swim to the surface, take a breath and plunge down again to find him. His hair drifted in the current. His lips were full; I thought he was smiling. He looked at me and beyond me. He reached out, fingers stretched wide to touch the world.

He had a huge erection and dark green pubic hair. Everywhere else his skin was smooth and hairless. When he kissed me, he shared his breath.

Later I filled the great claw-footed tub with steaming water and submerged myself in it. I touched my body and recalled the kisses of my green-haired friends—for a woman with green buds at the tips of her breasts had joined us.

I thought of fingers brushing me like water ferns and reeds; their slender tongues imparting their own wetness.

I called to the warm soapy water in the tub to come alive again and embrace me. *Water takes many forms.* But this time it stayed inert, simply water.

Life went on like this for several years, though a dopey boy called Trevor caused trouble.

"*The man in the woods! The man in the woods!*" Trevor had cried when he woke from an afternoon nap in a field and spotted me with my companion. The sight, it was said, drove him mad.

But my companion didn't have the slightest interest in Trevor or any of my associates. Until we met Rachel.

VII
BLANK SPACE

THINGS REMAIN CORDIAL WITH RORY. He even invites me to drop by again. I bring an article that Nao had written about my open house, thinking he'd find it entertaining. But he's in a foul mood when I arrive.

He complains that his friend's club opening has been delayed, and so are his expected sales. "But maybe those pieces are no good, not the way they are." He goes from one object to another, tinkering and talking. His agitation infects my own state of mind.

Oh yes, I know that doubt, that fussing.

There's that irksome section, the empty field in my painting. "Don't be so grumpy," I tell him. "Maybe we can help each other. I'm stuck myself, so I know what you're going through. I once asked an artist friend whether you disappeared if you walked past the vanishing point. Maybe I must answer that question before I finish this painting. But my friend said I was being silly. Do you think so?"

"No! But then, no one's ever been there to find out."

"What if any point can become a vanishing point? Is there a limit?"

"Fucked if I know," says Rory as he applies a monkey wrench to one of his mutated cars. "Isn't that maths you're talking about?"

"No, I never talk about maths."

52

I stop at one of his leather trees, and see that he's replaced the lining in the hollows. Now it's dark and soft. Thick. I put my fist into the hollow and spread my fingers through the fur. "This has changed," I say. "For the better."

"Yeah, that pink fun fur was tacky. Then I found some nice scraps at a stall."

"Why don't you bring your trees and things to my next open house?"

He looks at me, disgusted that I'd even suggest this. "Nah, they're not finished."

Getting Rory to do anything is like pushing that proverbial stone up a hill—am I really related to this guy?

"Mine weren't finished last time," I remind him. "But a few people came and *obviously* enjoyed it. I even got a good review. If you exhibit with me, people will take pleasure in your work and you'll get reviewed too. Hiding it in your garden won't do you much good."

"Pleasure, you say?" Rory looks up from what he's doing, smiling for the first time this evening. "Did the review refer to some very particular . . . *appreciation* of your work?"

"Yes, but in a discreet way. I wouldn't expect such discretion from a journo, but life has its surprises. I brought the review with me. Do you want to hear?"

"Yeah, go on." Rory gives another twist of his wrench.

I take the magazine out of my bag and read:

"She is resolutely unfashionable with her overtly figurative yet fanciful work and her cut-glass accent. But the most casual glance at Helen Vaughan's meticulously drafted people, creatures and flora—let alone the steely intensity and disquieting gaze of the artist herself—makes it clear she runs on the wild and dark side. This has drawn a strong and surprising response from some viewers . . . "

"'Steely intensity?'" Rory laughs. "D'ya mean like this?" He gives me a cross-eyed look.

"You're not too far off the mark," I tell him. For Nao's feature includes a picture of me half-scowling, half-smiling in front of a section of *Where the Places Meet*.

I give the photo a closer look. My skin is still smooth, but there's a suggestion of laughter lines at the corner of my eyes. Just enough for a touch of character, of maturity.

I've appeared as thirty-five for many years. The *changing* slows down deterioration. I was well past my twenties before I realised I didn't age in a normal way. Could it be two, three years since a transformation has taken place? This is the longest my companion has stayed away.

"And who wrote that pretentious rubbish?"

"Nao Harris."

"I could've guessed. Why would I want to bring my work somewhere just so some pretentious twat like Nao Harris can take the piss?"

"It's publicity. I can use it. So can you."

"Fuck publicity," Rory says. Then he gets out his blowtorch.

When I return home, I look again at that empty section. No matter how many details I fill that field with, it's still a blank space. Someone much more important still needs to go there.

This time she starts to take shape as I paint. She's walking away, across the meadow. Her face isn't visible, but I show it's Rachel from the way she holds herself, the squaring of her shoulders and the deep red of her hair escaping from under her hat. She's dressed in plain practical clothes, suitable for a long journey. There's no languor, no dreaminess, no suggestion she is leaving a scene of sensual indulgence. She's only leaving.

Where did she go to? After all these years I still don't know. I can only imagine.

And to extend that imagination, I must paint this part of the story from the *beginning,* from when I first met Rachel.

With this resolved, I go to bed. When I close my eyes I still see Rachel's image as I ease into sleep.

Soon I'm walking along a road. I think Rachel is just beyond a rise in the landscape.

I'm stepping over broad fissures in the tarmac. Goldenrod and fireweed, violets and lady slippers, daisies and buttercups spring from these cracks and line the roadside. I see ragweed and thistles in all stages of flower and seed and spiking. Spring violets, elderflowers, dandelions in yellow and white. A scent of thyme, rosemary and rotting leaves.

But as I walk, the colours start to drain away. Soon I'm surrounded by black and white, greyscale. Then nothing at all. No colour. I stop smelling the scents of dust and flowers. All sound is dampened along with the draining of colour. The cheeping of birds, the creeping of insects, the stirring of wind dwindles down with each step.

Now I hear nothing. I'm surrounded by *nothing.* It presses. It obliterates, until I'm not there.

I wake with an urge to jump out of my skin. It crawls as if insects with metal feet walk over it. I need to *change.* I need to be me, whatever that is. But in this dream I had ceased to be at all.

Ordinary humans have years to live with that fear of not-being, the blankest space imaginable. But this hits me all at

55

once, with concentrated force. This will happen to me if I go on as I am, without transforming. Without *him*.

I can't just lie here. I have to act. And all I can do now is get out of bed and paint again.

As I arrange my brushes and materials I remember Hopi's response to *Sprites* and the way it warmed me. I think of inner flesh with an abalone-shell sheen, and the scent of voluptuous flowers. Thinking of the flowers, I rummage in my trunk for mementos I can use to make them real. I remember gusts of intoxicating pollen, a sprinkling of seeds. The texture of supple bark on trees, the taste of their sap. I think very hard about places far from the desolate road I walked in my dream. Will I wander in those forests again?

I start to paint as the moon's light pours through the windows, touching each canvas with another palette of colours. Here is silver-washed purple and brown, then ivory and lemon petals spring open.

"Pieces of light," I whisper to myself. "Look for the pieces of light."

VIII
CATALYST

RORY HAS MADE HIMSELF PRESENTABLE this time. His t-shirt is clean. The grey in his hair shows as silver, so he must have washed it. He's regained his enthusiasm as he plumps the cushions on the armchairs and sofa. We've put out the tea and coffee and the wine. He nods with a smile as I expound on nineteenth-century salons.

People start arriving. Members of new indie bands slouch among arty locals and the scruffy denizens of the Belfry. One indie boy wears a t-shirt showing an AK-47 and the slogan 'Defend Williamsburg', crossed out and replaced with 'Defend Shoreditch?'

There are also a few people drawn by flyers at the more exclusive galleries.

I listen to snatches of conversation.

"Bit anachronistic, but what the fuck . . . "

"Art has no politics. It's just about looking."

"Wankers, most of 'em." Rory indicates our guests.

"I'm sure they're OK when you get to know them," I reply. "Maybe they put on airs and graces. But at heart, they want *colour* in their lives and beauty beyond the ordinary. Is that so bad?"

Rory scowls. "Colour? Beauty? Look at the state of that geezer with the lilac skinny jeans and the cheetah-print dishcloth on his head!"

"I've seen worse."

"So you're getting soft, Helen. I mean, look at the other twit in that t-shirt. It's not like there's been anything to defend in Shoreditch for years! Fuck it, I'm getting another beer."

He pushes past Nao as she makes her way towards us, accompanied by a tall man with pepper-and-salt hair. Just the way he carries himself proclaims quantities of money. I spent years among people like him so I can spot that confidence—calm rather than cocky. Flanking the gentleman is a slender young woman with an oval face and big brown eyes. Though she nods at their conversation, she's looking at the paintings.

Nao insists on hugging me. "Helen, I love the new elements, especially the flowers. A bit Judy Chicago, like *The Dinner Party*? I adored Judy when I was young and called myself a feminist! But these flowers seem *more* than three-dimensional. As if they're about to open and . . . oh look who's just come in. It's that girl from last time. The one who . . ."

"Yes, I must say hello to her. She's a bit shy, if you remember. Hi, Hopi."

As she walks past the paintings, Hopi keeps her arms straight along her sides, hands clenched. I smile at her and she turns an appealing pink, like the blush on an old variety of rose. I welcome her with wine and a plate of canapés. Hopi nods, looking at her feet. She reaches towards a canapé, then hesitates. "Listen, I'm really sorry about the other time."

"And I told you I was flattered! And much more, I was delighted. I talked about Rorschachs, but I aim for *more* than that. I'm trying to create visual catalysts."

Hopi nods. "I'm with you about that. But I still don't know if I'd want anyone doing . . . what I did to one of my installations. It's bad enough when people pop the bubblewrap, but anything else . . . It would break, know what I mean?"

"That's only an argument for using more durable materials, rather than prohibiting intense audience interaction." I put my arm around Hopi and this time she doesn't flinch. "Tell me, what's your real name?"

"Hopi *is* my real name, for fuck's sake." She removes herself out from under my arm. "My parents were a little *different*. OK, they were hippies. They were obsessed with Native American things though they're from Sheffield and never went anywhere near America." She expels a noisy breath of exasperation.

"Look, sorry if I just snapped at you," she adds quickly. "But I do get tired of people asking that. People took the piss at school all the time."

"You can do much worse than have hippies for parents. My stepfather was a *scientist*. You wouldn't want that."

"Is that so bad? Did he do experiments on you or something?"

"Yes, he most certainly did."

Hopi looks at me as if expecting to hear more, but I move her towards the paintings. She stops at *Sprites* and smiles as if she's bumped into an old friend. I'm pleased to see her reach out and place a fingertip where mother-of-pearl glistens between the female's legs. "It *is* wet," she says with wonder.

"So it is . . . " A tall black guy with a lithe dancer's body and a shaved head joins her. He extends his index finger, touching and drawing back, touching it again and again. He moves his hand with a languid grace, as if led by a melody. "This is powerful . . . "

"But I'm wondering . . . " Hopi takes a step back. "These are all rural scenes, yet you live in London. Where's the city? Where are the cities?"

"Do we need them?" the tall dancer asks.

"Perhaps we do," I say to him. "Hopi's right. I wouldn't be able to hold an event like this in the middle of the woods. Just look at all these people."

I scan the room as I consider the combinations and notice a slender man with close-cropped hair, the same shiny dyed black as Nao's, taking photos of paintings. He holds the camera up as if he's shielding himself. But when he puts it down and looks at the work with a naked eye, sweat starts to glisten on his forehead before he turns away.

"My ex-husband," says Nao behind me. "He'll give you bad reviews if I've been favourable. It's always been like that. And he was big on Brit Art, you see."

"So he's an art critic too?"

"I'd say he's just a general moaner and whinger. He whinges most about film, but every so often he does art just to annoy me. It's like a tomcat pissing and spraying to mark out his territory. I'll tell him to stop taking photos if you don't want to make a scene." She brandishes her wine bottle, ready for battle.

"Let him take photos. I don't mind." I listen, try to gauge the atmosphere. I see again the movement of that dancer's hand as he strokes my sprite . . . as if my companion's music animates it. My companion isn't here, but I once taped his music. He'd been too absorbed in pipe-playing to notice.

I find the tape in a box of old cassettes and put it on low. Though it's poor quality, it sounds just right as the reedy sound weaves under the conversations in the room.

I walk over to join a young man with blond dreadlocks who's looking at the Pan and Panisca statue next to the teapot on the table. His interest in the statue interests me. Close up I see he's not as young as I thought. The skin stretched across a sharp-featured expressive face is weathered and finely lined.

"Are you alright?"

"Yeah, just looking at this. I didn't think there were female Pans."

"The oldest Arcadian vision of Pan is much more varied. And more interesting. I don't see so much attraction in a hairy guy who always looks like a goat, do you?"

60

He chuckles as he picks up the statue and turns it around. "*She* doesn't look like a goat, does she, except for those little bumps on her head."

"Pan came in many forms . . . male and female, animal and human and what lies beyond that. Pan means 'all' or 'everything'. The Arcadians called him—or her, or *it*—lord of matter and the mingler of all things. The Christian devil was sometimes called 'lord of matter'. But what's wrong with *matter*? We're all made of matter, and it's what the ground beneath our feet is made of and even the air we breathe. It's what the world is made of."

The dreadlocked man hands the statue to me, but seems reluctant to part with it. "There are different kinds of matter, though. And what makes it *live*?" He shakes his head as if a troubling memory is coming back to him. "Sometimes I can't tell the difference. Sometimes it speaks to me and touches me."

"And is that so bad?"

"Bad isn't the word. But I can't say it's good. First time, I was at this outdoor rave with Rory and some other mates. I needed a piss so I walked into the woods on my own . . . I still heard voices, music and all. But where I was, everything went quiet. Then I heard other stuff. I heard the sap going through the trees and I could *taste* it. It was warm and it was like milk. It was disgusting. I heard twigs snapping, something was there, looming over me. Was it just a tree or what? I was afraid to look, but I had to."

"And what did you see?"

"I really can't remember. But it set something off. It's not just what I saw then, but what I *kept* seeing in everything else. Like that bowl of brown sugar with big crystals. I can look at that and the crystals are moving like worms. First I blamed it on the drugs, but it's not that."

He lapses into silence and stares at the statue, watching the way my hands cradle and touch it. When I hold it up towards him, his eager flow of words resumes. "Everything's got another shape in it and you're not sure which is real, the one on the surface or the one below. It took ages to get back to normal, and Rory's helped a lot. But what's so great about being normal? Going to a shitty job every day. Losing your imagination. So I've seen some scary stuff. But I remember wonderful things, like swimming in a lake just after a party, when the sun was about to rise, and the water seemed to be alive and making love to me . . . "

He puts his hand on over mine on the Panisca. He's not aware of it though. He closes his eyes and he smiles as if that water plays over him now.

When I hear someone talk this way, I always warm to them. I'm moved by the thought someone can be like me, in mind if not the physical ability to change. That's where I went wrong in the old days when I dallied mainly with gentlefolk. I need to find people who know my companion in some form, anyone who seeks him, even when they fear him.

I lean close to him and lower my voice. "That bit about the water . . . I've felt it, many times. Look at that painting called *Sprites*. If something's disorientating and you think you're losing your grip, you just have to stop fearing it. I can show you how. So can *she*." I stroke the neck and shoulders of my Panisca.

"What's this hippie shit you're on about?" I turn around to find Nao's ex behind me.

"Never mind. Me and . . . ."

"Jonny."

"Jonny and I were just having a chat here. And you are?"

"Justin. I write for *The Lads Bag* and *Film Week* and I'm on *Late Arts Review* . . . "

"What do you think of the paintings?" I put my question in quickly before this individual recites his entire CV to me. Jonny has already wandered off. I don't blame him.

"I've been commissioned to write about this event for the Late Arts website, and find it an interesting phenomenon. You've appeared out of nowhere and you're already creating a stir. That doesn't usually happen to an unknown artist. What makes you so special?"

"Am I being interviewed, Justin? Perhaps we can do it another time."

I'm trying to look past Justin to watch Hopi in a clinch with her new young man in front of *Sprites*, They're swaying in time with the pipes. Other people sway too and wind their way among the massive canvasses. People who had arrived separately now touch and whisper as they view the paintings. The air itself is warming, acquiring new layers of scent and sound. In some corners laughter rises.

Things are getting lively. I just need to extricate myself from Justin, though Nao is glaring at him as if she has plans to send him packing very soon.

"Ms Vaughan? Are any of these paintings for sale? My daughter and I are very interested in one."

It's Nao's Important Person, flanked by the serious young woman. He hands me a card. With a glance I see he's Franklin Forbes, a big art collector with a gallery in central London.

After some small talk, we discuss a price for *Sprites*. He wants to take the painting away now. The dark-eyed daughter takes little interest in the mercantile proceedings, though she nods in approval once the sale is agreed and tucks a piece of paper in the frame. SOLD. She waits by it until the two blokes turn up to move it.

Hopi and her partner are agitated at this change, as if something precious is about to be lost forever. I go over to reassure them. "Look at this *new* painting, *Where the Places Meet*. Imagine what these places are. I've added those big flowers. But

63

maybe it needs much more. Hopi suggested urban images, for example."

Hopi's new friend smiles and tells me his name. *Ben.* He strokes the fleshy petals I'd painted a few nights ago. Hopi begins stroking too, her other arm around his waist.

"What technique did you use?" she asks. "These are wonderful to touch too."

"Follow those red veins," I suggest, "See the other layers. And all this . . . " I caress a stamen that I'd clothed in old skin I sloughed off at another party many years ago. It is covered in dense, very short hair; velvet that can't be woven. The sensation sparks a vivid memory: what it was like to be in that skin, and feel so many fingers running over it.

The old velvet on the canvas yields to my touch and moistens. I extend my fingers and a piece of another world fills them. It coats my hand with powdery rust-coloured pollen that releases a scent sharp like fresh sweat, tempered by allspice. I draw it into my lungs and laugh. I rub my hands together and the pollen turns to a grainy yet slippery oil.

"Hey cool!" exclaims Ben. "I was telling Hopi your paintings are full of colours and shapes I'd love to dance to. But there's even more to them . . . "

"So try some of this!" I rub it onto his smooth-shaven head. Hopi clasps my hand and then brings her fingers to her mouth and licks off the oil. Then she kisses me. The three of us look at each other and draw closer. A woman as opulent as those massive blossoms in my painting is now applying the pollen between her breasts.

Another woman has joined us, bringing the Shoreditch-defending indie boy with her. She seems older than the others, older than I'm meant to be yet somehow ageless. Her body is a graceful pear-shape in well-cut jeans. Her crisp white shirt

64

bears a trace of rust colour. Her hair in its single plait is close to pure white, with only a hint of darker hair in its depths.

"This reminds me of the old days. We called these 'happenings'." A dimple appears in one round cheek. I dab some pollen there.

"So what's happening?" asks indie-boyfriend.

"What we *want* to happen," I say.

"That's the spirit!" The white-haired woman guffaws. She must think I'm going for some 1960s retro irony. I join in the laughter, though I really meant what I said.

The music is getting louder. Surely it's ringing between my ears. I stretch across the canvas and close my eyes. Many hands start to explore me as if I'm another work of art. A slither and sleekness of long hair over my skin, more velvet from the touch of a tongue.

Hopi is laughing, a throaty chuckle deepening into an all-out belly laugh. It's the first time I've heard her laugh like this.

There are giggles from other people, intakes of breath. Exclamations.

One laugh is drawn out very long, and rises until it's more like a cry. There's another sound close to a sob. "What are you doing?"

Another voice. "I'm going home!"

My back is still touched by canvas, but I'm breathing in the scent of the forest I've painted. My skin is prickling and tingling as if it wants to move, to spread further to catch more feeling. This is the point where it begins, when it's time to *change*. But my companion isn't here and Rory isn't either. I stretch my hand out to capture more pollen. If I can't change, this will help me *feel* like I'm doing it.

When Jonny comes over, I place some on his lips.

IX
THE TWO MAGICIANS

"WHAT'S THIS FATUOUS 1970S NONSENSE? This could be an album cover for some dreadful heavy-metal band."

I'm reading Justin's write-up on the *Arts Review* website.

It's late in the afternoon. Jonny is still sleeping. Empty bottles, soiled plates and items of clothing are scattered around the room. There are rust-coloured smudges on the floor in front of *Places.* But the distinctive scent of the pollen is gone.

If those smudges on the floor show that something from *there* has come over *here,* a slating from Justin hardly matters. But I read on, as you do.

> "'Gothic post-Stuckism?' But you can't be 'post' to something that is entirely reactionary. And what of those comparisons to Richard Dadd? This only makes me want to take an axe with the aim of consigning these paintings to the same fate as Dadd's unfortunate Dad."

There's a photo of me holding my statue, finger on the Panisca's breast.

I think I hear Jonny stirring in the bedroom. We'd ended up in the bath last night, and he was an imaginative lover. With some tutoring, he may learn not to fear what he sees in a bowl of sugar.

Nao rings. "Don't worry about Justin's review, Helen. I warned you about the backlash."

"I don't mind at all. I've had a lot of emails asking about the next open house."

"Ah! Glad to hear it's turned out to be a *good* bad review. Sometimes they work more magic than praise. Like that photo of you playing with that statue. A bit kitsch maybe, but some people will find it intriguing. Perhaps I can write a bad review for you too."

Nao laughs, a note of hysteria entering her giggles. "Of course, I'm only joking."

Was she calling my Pan and Panisca *kitsch*? Maybe grumpy old Rory has a point about Nao after all. I stroke the smooth marble, admire the taut and straining limbs of the trio.

I was seventeen when Rachel gave it to me. Rachel had been a year younger, but she seemed to know much more. She often went away with her father and came back with beautiful things: little fur-lined jackets, a lacy confection of a hat.

She spoke of visits to an unmarried aunt in London who was something of a bluestocking, and her visits to booksellers where she bought volumes of banned French poets. She spoke of theatres and concert halls. She proclaimed her fascination for the world of cities and culture, her desire to encounter all that was strange and unusual.

So perhaps I shouldn't have been surprised when she expressed an interest in me.

I had been content to ramble in the woods and play with my companions. How could anything compare to my secret swims, or the breath of wind sprites on my bare skin? But for the first time an ordinary girl offered something that *they* couldn't.

I jumped at the chance when Rachel invited me to her home.

She took me to her room, where she showed me her clothes hanging in a vast walk-in cupboard. There were velvets, linens, cottons and silks. Every shade of blue, purple, yellow and red. But most of all, I was drawn by greens that could have grown in the woods I roam. I'd not seen anything like it. Though the Rosses looked after me well, they were practical farming folk who didn't concern themselves with fashion. Until then I had shared their view. Clothes were simply there to keep me warm, or for removing when the situation warranted it.

"Why don't you try something?" Rachel urged. "You are dark and exotic, like an Italian or Arabian princess. You'd look wonderful in that green."

As we undressed and dressed, I watched my friend, fascinated by the red hair under her arms and the dark red hair on her head that set off her fair, milky skin. With her red and white colouring, she was a fair apple of a girl.

Rachel wore green as well, a darker bottle green.

"Think of how we look together!" Rachel put her arm next to mine. The fairness of her skin had a pearl-like glow. My own skin was a warm tan, like polished wood. As we contemplated our arms side by side, I noticed a sculpture on her cluttered table-top. It was half-covered by a scarf: a young man with compact curly horns and a powerful upper body, and a woman who also had the horns showing through her thick hair. He had his arm around a slender young shepherd, whose legs were also intertwined with those of the female Pan.

"What's this?"

"It's an old thing my aunt gave me. It's only a copy. Of course, my parents shouted about it being obscene. But my aunt said it was *classical* culture and classics are my best subject. I'm very good at Latin and Greek. My parents hired a special tutor for me, but

68

now they worry that my scholarly pursuits go too far. They only wanted me to pick up a smattering to make me a cultivated wife."

"Cultivated? Like a well-trimmed hedge or shrub?"

Rachel gave a snort.

"Exactly!" Then she put her arm around me and whispered: "Tell me, what do you do in the woods on your own? Why don't you take me along when it gets warm again?"

When we set off a few weeks later, Rachel said: "I heard a story about a naked man playing with you in the woods and terrifying a little boy. But I don't believe it."

"Perhaps it is true. I do have this rather odd friend who appears now and then."

"Ha! Helen, I like your sense of humour." Rachel put her arm through mine as we walked along the old Roman road through the wood, a green avenue between high red banks and beech trees. Through the trees we caught glimpses of rolling hills and fields on one side, the sea on the other.

I took Rachel to my favourite place, where the road goes up a gentle slope and widens into an open space almost surrounded by thick undergrowth. A pillar of stone with a foreign inscription stood in the clearing.

Rachel peered at the pillar's carved inscription. She stroked its worn angles and ridges as if she drew its meaning through her fingertips. "I can just about read the Latin," she said. "To Nodens, god of the abyss—or perhaps *void*—and regeneration, Flavius has erected this pillar on account of the marriage that he saw beneath the shade."

"Marriage? This is hardly a church," I laughed.

"He wouldn't mean that *literally*. But who really knows what this Flavius fellow had seen? Some people say this spot is haunted."

"Maybe that's why no one else comes here except for me—and now you."

We drank and ate our cheese, bread and meat. "What do we do now?" Rachel asked when we were full with our food. Her eyes were half closed; her smile, languid. "Eating outdoors makes me think of family picnics. We always played games afterwards. Some of them were quite dull. I never liked croquet. But I liked hide and seek, and also blind man's bluff. It was fun to get spun around and then not know where I really am. And when I opened my eyes, the world didn't look the same."

"Yes, I know exactly what you mean!"

Rachel stood up and closed her eyes. "Let's go! You can start with me."

"No, I have a better idea," I suggested. "We can do it together, we'll both be lost."

And so we held hands and closed our eyes. We went round and round, gathering momentum, gathering force. Spinning, spinning. Eyes closed, seeing sparks behind my lids. Rachel's hands gripped mine.

When I opened my eyes, everything was a blur as sky, green growth and earth flowed together. My hands were warm against Rachel's. There was no end to my hand, no finish to Rachel's. A single joining of skin and flesh bound us together, locking us as we spun faster.

Nature decrees that the force of our spin should drive us apart. But we were drawing closer. Rachel's hair was in my mouth, surrounding me in a dark curtain of red.

When she let go, we didn't fall, but came closer to each other. *His* hands pushed gently on my back, his dark matted hair mingling with Rachel's silky red. Across from me, his female reflection grinned. Her elongated eyes flashed with green fire as she flicked a red tongue over berry-stained lips.

70

Then he left us, letting us fly apart. As we hit the grass, we shrieked and giggled. And Rachel sprawled on the grass, smiling up at me.

That's what I paint now: my memory of Rachel as she stretched on the grass that first time.

I lay on each stroke as if it will bring Rachel back, or take me to where she went. I paint as if combining the right colours will again shift the barrier that had lifted last night.

"Coffee, Helen?" There's a shout from the kitchen, accompanied by rattling cups.

I've been so involved in painting, I haven't noticed that Jonny is up and dressed.

When he joins me, it's clear that he's thinking about more than coffee. He looks at Rachel; looks at me. Though I've not yet painted us together, I know he sees that too.

"No coffee now, Jonny. Just relax while I carry on with this . . ."

The whole land smelled like the wine we were drinking, of crushed grape and trampled grass. We stretched on the hillside, half in sun and half in shadow. Rachel's face was veiled by the shade, while patterns of sun covered the rest of her. I hitched my skirt up higher to expose my legs to it. Rachel did the same.

I shielded my eyes with my hand, and looked towards hills covered with corn and barley. The sea glinted beyond. Though the air around us was still, a constant rustle and whisper moved through the ground and grass.

In the sky a large bird, a hawk or even an eagle, glided and circled. Could it be watching us on the hill, the two young women with wine-flushed skin and dishevelled hair?

Or it could be searching for prey. Though I had been sated with our lunch, a pang of overwhelming hunger assailed me as I imagined its desire for warm flesh and hot blood . . .

I sat up. "Rachel," I started to say. Then I saw that she had drifted into sleep. Her arms were flung above her head, so she was stretched out to her full length upon the hill. Her head was turned to the side towards me. The curves of her breasts swelled over her dress, glistening with a light dew of sweat.

Desire as sharp as the brief pang of hawkish hunger hit me. But this didn't go away.

I had never felt such an ache before. Though my companion had sometimes come to me in womanly form, it was a new sensation to feel desire for a young woman like myself.

I stroked Rachel's cheek, a curl that had fallen across her face. I drew my fingers through the rest of her hair. Sparks of electricity snapped under my fingers. Holding my breath, I stroked the rise of her breast. I leaned over and licked her ear.

Rachel sighed and stirred, her lips lifted in a curve.

Encouraged, I stroked the sun-heated flesh of her thighs. I stopped, and waited.

Rachel opened her eyes, "Carry on Helen, for goodness' sake."

I straddled her and unbuttoned her dress. She reached up and undid mine too. She smiled as her white hands spanned the golden-brown of my breasts. "I told you we look good together," she said. "Do you think anyone can see us?"

"I don't think so," I answered. Before I bent down to kiss her, I took one last look at the sky where that eagle rode the winds.

"I can see you," I whisper to Rachel and my younger self in the painting. "I see your skin against mine." My brush describes the curve of her breasts, the cream and rose of her skin. The arch of a back, crushed grass. Curve on curve, lips parting.

"God, that's beautiful!" Jonny gasps.

"God has nothing to do with it."

Afterwards, Rachel and I went to a nearby pond and splashed water on ourselves. Though the afternoon's heat had waned, we were still hot and sticky with its pastime. I watched our reflections, our hair mussed with bits of grass, lips red from so much kissing and sucking. Our splashing disturbed the surface and broke our images into pieces.

Rachel sighed. "Helen, I don't want to go home. My parents won't be back until late, so we can go into the town over the hills, to the public house. I've been there with my father after the market."

I held onto Rachel's arm. "Wait," I urged. "Keep still."

Our reflection came together again, rippling.

"The men are all looking at us!" Rachel whispered when we en-tered the pub.

Indeed, they were. There were some fine youths there. I'd never paid much attention to the young men in our own vil-lage. Perhaps I wouldn't have paid much notice to those here, but Rachel's gaze inspired me to look again.

The few women in the pub also looked at us. But I met suspicious stares with a smile. It was the way *he* made me smile, and the light of it spread to them. It was my first inkling that lessons I learned in the forest could be useful far beyond it.

Musicians near the bar started playing—guitars, a fiddle and accordion. One song led to another. They were mostly about harvests and drinking, something about a blacksmith. I enjoyed watching Rachel as she listened with her head tilted with an aloof, amused air. But she couldn't keep up the pose of a sophisticated city girl. Soon she was joining in when she knew the words. *"With his hammer in his hand, he looks so clever!"*

The singer introduced the next song. "Here's another tune about a blacksmith! But it's the lady who's not the marrying kind this time . . . " He began:

> *The lady sits at her own front door,*
> *As straight as a willow wand,*
> *And by there come a lusty smith,*
> *With his hammer in his hand,*
> *Crying "Bide lady bide,*
> *For there's a nowhere you can hide,*
> *For the lusty smith will be your love,*
> *And he will lay your pride . . . ."*

But she replies:

> *"Away, away you coal-black smith, I'd rather be dead and cold,*
> *Than a husky, dusky, musty, fusky lusty coal-black smith,*
> *Me maidenhead should have . . . "*
> *And she became a tree, that tree it was a pine,*
> *And he became an ivy vine, that round her limbs did twine.*

74

Long ago I had dreamed of great vines coming out of the ground and embracing me. And now I was listening to a song that expressed this dream, and much more.

The transformations of the lady and the lusty smith enthralled me:

So she turned into a full dress ship,
And she sailed all over the sea,
Ah, but he became a bold captain,
And aboard of her went he . . .

She turned into a mare, and he a golden saddle. The lady turned into a sheep; he became a big horny ram. *"And soon he was upon her."*

Next to me Rachel scowled and fidgeted.

She became a bottle of wine, filled with sparkling red,
And he became a big thick cork and gained her . . .

This last verse was greeted with shouts, "That's a way! Nothing like a big thick cork."

"Better thick than long, that's what me wife says!"

"I don't like this song." Rachel exclaimed. "Imagine! What if the smith in our village wanted us? He's old and fat. He smells and hair grows out of his ears. And what if he kept after us and did those things and had his way even when he's told 'no'. How horrid!"

"I wouldn't want to be harried by him either, but this song's not about him. If the smith can keep changing himself, would he be old and smelly? He'd be as handsome as he wants to be, or you would have him be."

"But . . ."

"It's a contest between two wilful people, like a game. And don't you like games?"

75

So she turned into a mulberry tree,
A mulberry tree in the wood,
But he came forth as the morning dew,
And sprinkled her where she stood.

Rachel jabbed me with her elbow. "That's disgusting!"

"No, *no*. Imagine the sun is coming up and the morning dew glistens everywhere, all over you and on every blade of grass . . . "

"Helen, you're a very strange girl." But Rachel eyed me thoughtfully, as if "strange" wasn't such a bad thing to be in this little village where nothing ever happened.

She became a glove, a glove all made of fur,
And he became a cold, cold man, and put his hand in her.

Now people added their own verses. *"She became a house, a house along the way,"* a woman announced, with a triumphant toss of her head.

The singer replied: *"And he became a wayfarer, and entered her by day."*

"A star! She became a star! A star in the night." I shouted. How could anyone surpass a star?

"And he became a thundercloud, and muffled her out of sight."

"A hot griddle!" The publican's wife sang out.

So she became a hot griddle and he became a cake,
And anyways she turned herself the blacksmith was her mate.

When people ran out of new verses, the fiddle player drew out the chords and the singer crooned:

So the lady she ran into her chamber,
And she changed into a bed,

Ah, but he became a green coverlet,
And he gained her maidenhead.

"Of course. Of course he gets what he wants in the end. What do you expect?"

"Rachel, I told you, it's only a song. And why would the lady turn into a bed if she didn't want him at all? She was testing him to see if he's really so clever. And maybe the story hasn't really ended, even though this singing of it has."

"What do you mean?"

"She can change into something else again. This story has no end."

The old song is in my head and it drives my brush, the transformations flowing from it. It is no longer a quaint little folk song, or the allegedly rape-glorifying ditty that offended my lovely friend Rachel.

I can't paint fast enough to show this attraction and change. Shapes shimmer and converge, there is fur and hair and skin and scales. There is water, air and light and everything that grows from the earth. Long grass moves and whispers in the hot winds of August; pale and dark forms twist and turn. An arched back, exposed beasts, a lean flank flexes and plunges, a mouth open with cries that rise over the field and turn into black birds. Curves and circles, deep hollows and the thrust of heat. There is male and female, and something beyond both. I am painting to the heart of matter itself, matter continually bending, smearing, fucking itself, making itself *more*.

"Jeez, Helen, what the hell is *that*?"

The ragged tone of Jonny's voice makes me pause.

But I'm sure he won't go . . . like those others. I remember how he talked about making love with the water and what we got up to last night in the bath. He's not like those apoplexy-prone Victorians, keeling over or topping themselves for no reason. Swanleigh, Collier-Stuart and the rest of them.

Or Meyrick. I had believed that *he* was different. Curious, creative, not spoiled by public school. But again, that was a long time ago. He was still a good Victorian boy at heart. The authorities said Meyrick had experienced "a total collapse of the nervous system" at the time of his death. But that happened after I left Buenos Aires. Perhaps he'd sampled the wrong local herbs or hit the absinthe too much.

I try to soothe Jonny. "It's nothing you need to fear."

I return to Rachel and add a touch of lilac, red fuzz under a plump uplifted arm, deep shadow at the junction of her legs, a glisten of dew. I pause to consider what goes next.

"Don't stop, Helen!"

I glance back to see Jonny stretched on the armchair, like Rachel in my painting. He is stroking himself through his light-weight army trousers, but he doesn't seem to be aware of it. He is focused entirely on me, Rachel, my companion . . . just like Hopi when she pressed herself against *Sprites*.

I return to my work as requested. "I'm only making it last. Every brushing is slow, and spreads this hot, hot golden light all over you. And imagine you're stretched out on that field and every blade of grass is a little tongue. Think of where they kiss you."

No sound but the long, lingering strokes of my brush.

Then I switch to short, hard strokes. There's a gasp behind me, a low moan.

I'm breathing as hard as Jonny as my brush spreads light on Rachel's skin. She lifts her hips towards it.

Another loud gasp sounds behind me.

"We're getting there Jonny." Then I start to sing:

He became a field,
And she became the sun
And spread her warmth all over him . . .

This was a version I later sang to Rachel, though the order of the words was different.

And she became a field,
And he became the sun,
And spread his warmth all over her.

Rachel's eyes were closed, a faint smile showed she didn't mind this verse so much.

I shaded my eyes with my hand and saw it there again, the great eagle-bird riding the currents of air. Then it swooped down.

I moved my hand further up her forearm, under her sleeve. Her lips parted in response, her eyes stayed closed.

The bird in the sky was growing larger. It had golden-brown feathers and a white-crested head. It was coming straight towards us. It was only a bird. But look at that beak, those claws. It was bigger than any bird I've seen, and still it grew.

Its eyes held a cutting intelligence as it banked with its wings before landing. The bird pulled its outstretched claws back at the last moment. It landed on my chest, wings folded beneath it to cushion the impact of talons.

Now open, Rachel's eyes were wide and startled. But she reached out and stroked the wings. The bird's chest feathers against me were soft and downy, while the pinions of its wings were stiff and almost, it seemed, as sharp as its claws.

It was heavy upon me, solid and warm. I stroked it too, and it nestled closer into the curve of my body and the curve of Rachel's. When it spread its wings to cover us both, its claws didn't hurt us. For it was already changing.

Its form flowed and extended, brushing us with a succession of textures: plush and velvet, brittle like straw, a rasp like a kitten's tongue. I lost track of the creature's motions as it took on elements of man and woman, the bird it had once been.

And it was already leaving that form behind, embracing a multitude of others in fleeting transformations. I was fascinated. In Rachel's face there was terror, an echo of my own fascination. Her face underwent as many changes as the being that eventually stood in front of us. Her hand clutched mine.

The creature's flesh felt damp, a smoothness that verged on slimy. Then its touch was cool. No feathers, not much hair either.

It lengthened and smiled at us. It became a man, a tall man with wings that surrounded us, brushing against my legs.

"An angel!" All fear fled from Rachel.

"No, no! That's no angel. It's *him*."

As if he wanted to make that clear to Rachel, the wings shrunk into his back.

What *does* one do? Make introductions?

I loved her for not yielding to terror. And he saw her bright curiosity and desire for difference.

When he got on his feet he stood over a head higher than either of us. He was pale, with the pallor of the moon when a wisp of cloud passes over it. His hair was golden-brown and his eyes were too, long and slanted and penetrating as his touch. His fingers were long, ending with golden nails that reflected the sun. They were square, then curved down to sharp points.

Rachel was staring at him with her lips parted. He let her gaze move over him.

She whispered to me. "He has lips you want to eat like fruit."

I paint the fruit that was his lips, and show what it was like to lap its juice. "Jonny, this isn't just a funny fancy of a painting. I'm showing you that these things happened to me. And something even better can happen to us both. To all of us, to those who want it. People get frightened though. They're alone in the woods, there's the crack of a twig and they just run. But the secret lies in *dancing*, and moving with the world as it lurches out of shape. See my companion with the golden eyes as he comes to us? He's not finished yet. He is *never* finished. See how he moves his all-shape body as earth, sea and sky mix their melodies."

I half-speak, half-sing. I flex and extend my voice, stroking him with it. "I wish you could have met Rachel—and that you can meet *him*. He taught me many things. He showed me how to look and touch as we brought Rachel in to dance between us."

"Dance?" Jonny's hoarse voice interrupts. "How did Rachel dance with you? And *between* you?"

"It's how you dance to the music of your blood and body when it is stroked and stroked again. Every inch of skin touched and kissed and licked. How she moved and laughed!" My own laugh escapes from deep in my throat as I paint faster and the colours spatter. I sway with Rachel's movements as I remember. A blob of aquamarine slithers down my breast. Streaks of crimson intermingle and combine with the aquamarine. I add viridian.

Though we're not yet touching, Johnny and I dance together too. If we keep dancing, it will bring my companion closer. I blend the colours to a mist. And then a hand is thrust through it, rending it with sharp-tipped fingers. A slender leg extended, he's emerging. His eyes are narrowed in laughter; a grin curves his wide mouth. And in his other hand, he carries his pipes.

I reach out to him. I hear his music and my voice joins it in a song without words. But my companion again looks to a place far in the distance. Is it past the meadow, past the forest? I hesitate with my brush above the spot where that place can be and bring it down hard. And then *he* sees me. And Jonny.

There is a groan behind me. "Jonny?" I turn. Jonny is slumped and motionless, his eyes open and glassy, staring straight ahead.

"Oh *shit*, not again."

X
WHEN THE LIGHT GOES OUT

JONNY IS BARELY BREATHING. After a while, I can get him to move. If I direct him, he is able to walk. So he is alive. There'll be no repeat of all that fuss that happened over a century ago when gentlemen who visited my salon topped themselves one after another. "The West End Horrors", the tabloids called it. I dealt with that. It was easy when they had no evidence against me, but it would be more difficult now. Everything is more difficult now. Changing names, changing identities. A lot of trouble.

"Jonny, you'll be fine. I know you're made of stronger stuff than those toffs from way back when. You've come close to *him* without knowing it. That's why you were drawn to my statue. But what will I do with you now? I don't even know where you live."

I pace the floor. Then I snap my fingers. "You're Rory's mate! I'll just phone Rory and he'll sort it out."

Rory comes over straight away. Though I've cleaned up Jonny a bit, I haven't dressed. Rory stares at me, but it certainly isn't with desire. I throw on a dressing gown.

"He's able to walk, but I guess he's not himself just yet. Maybe if you had a word, Rory. You're an old friend, aren't you?"

"We travelled together in the 90s. For fuck's sake, Helen, what did you to do him?"

"Nothing. I was just painting. And he was watching me paint. We were kind of . . . flirting with each other."

"Helen! I can imagine what that involves."

"Well, you did have your chance."

"And from the looks of Jonny, I'm more than glad I didn't take it."

"As I said, I didn't harm a hair on his head. I never do. I am not a violent person, though some have implied otherwise."

"Some? Who?"

"It's a long story, and I'll be happy to tell it to you. If you're willing to listen."

"I guess I'll have to, won't I? But first things first . . . " He gives Jonny a hug and brushes the hair away from his face. "What's with you, mate? This ain't good, you know that."

With a wary glance at me, he guides Jonny to the door.

As the lift clanks down and the front door slams I turn back to my painting. I told Jonny that the secret lies with dancing. If he'd stayed longer I would have shown him. I would have shown how Rachel danced between us, and with us.

We were under the trees near the Roman monument. Rachel's head was on my lap, her hair fanning out in russet waves over my belly and legs. The shadow patterns on her face shifted with the leaves above us.

"Helen, Helen, today we will begin to make your friend happy."

He scratched that long gold fingernail between her breasts, until it disappeared under her clothing. She put her hand on his arm, to stroke it, but he shrugged it off gently.

"Lie still. Let me flow over you like water with no shore or coastline, no bank or boundary," he murmured in his rich voice.

I undid her buttons.

"Don't rush. Linger."

Rachel sighed, flinging her arms and legs wide. Vines with smooth, shining leaves grew out of the ground and wound around her limbs, holding her ready.

He kissed her belly, snaked his tongue into her naval and pushed. Rachel gave a surprised, breathy shout. Then he disappeared under her skirts. I didn't see what he was doing. But I heard Rachel's cries mixing with laughs; watched her twist and turn.

"Do it, now with your long, long tongue. Around the tops of my legs then in, and in . . . "

A note came from the sky, another from the stream, a succession of notes came from the rustle of leaves and the cries of animals. The notes moved inside us, insistent.

We fell upon each other, with mouths and fingers.

"Helen, your eyes have changed colour. They are green! *Very* green, with flecks of purple." She drew my face down towards her, closer. My eyes were brown, not green. I first thought she was simply intoxicated, seeing colours that weren't there. I didn't realise much more was about to change.

He released my hair from its French plait. It tumbled all over her, loose and thick. Its strands turned into black ivy that ran in tendrils over her body and intimately touched her.

She asked me for explanations. She was always waiting for me, wanting me to take her to him. Even when it grew colder, she wanted to go into the woods. He would keep us warm, he would make us burn.

She usually walked in front of me as we went to meet him. I watched her hips sway, side to side, a little forward. Already anticipating him, moving towards his touch.

I would put my hands on her hips, feeling how they moved under her woollen clothes.

"I like that, Helen. You can hold me this way when the three of us are together, and keep holding me when I can't stand up any longer."

She usually left first when we finished. I remember watching as she walked away from us on a late autumn day just as it grew dark, the damp air smoky from burning leaves. Though Rachel was in a hurry to get home this time, there was still a sway to her hips. Then she passed over the crest of a rise, and was gone from our sight.

Rachel's parents had encouraged our friendship, assuming I would inherit Dr Raymond's money some day. But they also wanted Rachel to make a suitable match and to marry. They introduced her to a succession of sons of the more prosperous farmers, and those from families bearing minor titles.

Around this time, my companion stopped coming to us.

This had happened before, I tried to assure Rachel. I don't know where he goes. He never tells me.

His response to a question would be a laugh, a wicked kiss or a play on those damn pipes. Sometimes I thought he did those things to distract me, other times he seemed to offer the music or the kisses as explanations. I would listen, trying to find a key in the sequence of notes, the vibrations of sound as they touched my ears. Or was it in the twist of his tongue as it touched me in so many other places?

His absence grew longer. Rachel was losing patience, and even I began to fret. It became too cold to go to the woods without him to warm us, so we devised rituals to invoke him indoors. We burned candles and whispered pleas to the Pan and Panisca, we dressed up and undressed. Though our efforts ended with the two of us acting out the pleasures of our out-door encounters, we were both left unsatisfied.

Then she engaged the boys chosen by her parents in similar play. She insisted on telling me the details: "It was no good, Helen. He was so clumsy. He just put it in and out and barely touched me. I licked him but he wouldn't lick me as I asked. Then he told me I was disgusting and would never make a wife with such behaviour. *Afterwards.*"

She laughed, but the laughter became more and more bitter. She often had dark circles under eyes and she grew thin.

It seemed as if something had been extinguished in her.

Finally, Rachel turned her frustration on me. We were standing near the Roman column, huddled in our coats and gloves under the fine rain.

"Helen, what have you done to me? Why did I go into the woods with you? You've ruined me! I'll never enjoy being with a normal man, or live a normal life. You and your *friend* have turned me into a freak!" She began to weep, with great heart-broken sobs.

Rachel had enjoyed being with us. She wanted something different, and different was what she found. While I was used to rejection from Dr Raymond and others, I didn't expect this from Rachel. It hit me like a blow. Then I rallied against the injustice of her accusations.

"We 'ruined' you for what? Marriage to someone you don't like? Marriage to a man who can't satisfy you? Have I ruined you for a life of drudgery and mediocrity? Well, good!"

The venom in my voice surprised me. I didn't intend to argue like this. When I saw Rachel with all her light gone, I only wanted to get it back for her. Now I was too angry.

"What do you call this, Helen? Living in a little village where nothing of interest happens, except for romps in the woods with God-knows what kind of . . . I want to live, I want to go places, I want to go to the theatre and talk about books and things that matter."

"And do you do that with the company you're keeping now?"

"No, of course not. That's why I'm going away soon. I'll go to London or Paris. Or even America. But before I go . . . I want to see *him* one more time. And I'll do it without your help."

"I wish you luck. Give him my regards. Meanwhile, why don't you teach your young men some manners instead of blaming me for their failures? Or shall I teach them for you?"

"No, no! Get away from me, Helen. Don't ever speak to me again. You're *foul*."

I watched her as she walked away. I almost shouted for her to come back, to talk more. Maybe I wanted to apologise for yelling at her. But I knew Rachel wasn't someone who'd turn her head at a shout. She was proud and stubborn, just as I liked her.

I wasn't there when Rachel left for good. I only know the stories told by people in the village. A boy claimed he saw her disappear in broad daylight while walking in a field. An old farmer said he saw that too.

This is what I try to capture in the painting. If I could have recorded the scene on film, I'd be playing and replaying the sequence. But I can only try to summon it in my mind. She occupies the space; now the space is empty. They intersect, and for a time both are true. Then she's gone.

Did it start with a shred light in a hidden part of a forest or a forgotten part of London? Or perhaps she followed a trembling shadow in the grass. *"I slip through the boundaries between the now and then, the here and there."* That's what he told us one afternoon. It didn't make sense to me, but Rachel had nodded.

Or she could have simply walked down a hill and kept walking. I've seen her do *that*. Rachel said there were places she wanted to go to. So maybe she just walked until she reached a railway station and caught a train to London.

Later I looked for Rachel in London and in all the places I thought she could be. So did my companion. And for all those clever-dick tricks of his, he couldn't find her either, though he said he might have seen her once.

He'd wandered into a city; I didn't recognise the name he gave it. He saw a woman walking down a silent street in the rain, familiar red hair spilling out the hood of her cloak. But when she turned and lifted that hood for a moment, he wasn't sure if he saw a face.

I only show her from the back as I draw. She's going away and there's no reason for her to turn. When she vanishes her outlines will fade until she becomes a mere smear of shadow on the grass. And then, nothing.

I have a quick try on a smaller canvas already painted with a background. I splash an impression of Rachel over it with thinned-out paint that lets winter weeds and damp earth show through.

No, you can do better than that with Photoshop.

I put down my palette and wander about, looking at the other scenes for clues.

Finally I sit down and turn my sculpture over a few times in my lap. The Pan is laughing in his merry way. The Panisca is offering her breast to the shepherd, with a look of tenderness on her face. She is both calm and wise, yet there are flames of passion in those blind marble eyes.

That young shepherd between them . . . Each time I look, his expression is different. Sometimes he's enjoying himself, his lips parted in pleasure. Another time he returns both the passion and compassion in the female Pan's eyes. It appears he has learned something from her, and I wonder what that is.

Today he seems worried. I put him back on the table.

I walk back and forth as I peer at Rachel, frozen in her own walk.

The bell rings. If it's Rory, perhaps he can advise me again.

"Jonny's got all his functions back OK," Rory announces as he lurches into my flat. "He's walking and talking."

"That's *excellent* news."

"But he's not saying much that makes sense. Keeps talking about 'a man in the woods'. But he wasn't near any woods, was he?" Rory paces the room and picks up the Pan and Panisca statue. He glares at it, as if the object is responsible for Jonny's state. But when he looks closer at the Panisca, Rory's expression softens. He sets the statue down gently.

"He was here with you, after all. Was he on something . . . that smelly stuff that got everyone off their faces at the showing? I had to leave because my hay fever was playing up. But what happened with Jonny?"

"What do you think? We talked about Arcadian myths and bad acid and seeing things. He had interesting ideas. We just got on with each other."

"I *bet*." Rory snorts and shakes his head. "Jonny. He took drugs. We all did while we were travelling. Ecstasy, acid, you name it. It was just *fun* for me. I thought it was expanding my mind, but I didn't *need* it. But maybe it still fucks Jonny up. His mum thinks so. I've just had a word with her. Poor Jonny. He did seem to be sorting himself out. He had a new job at a garage and he was doing alright. I hope he'll forget about that 'man in the woods'. Maybe he should stay at mine for a while. I'll give him a ring tomorrow."

"I think Jonny was talking about my painting. There's a man in the woods there. Would *you* like to meet him? I think you'll get on better."

Rory shakes his head. "Helen, is that what you think about at a time like this?" His voice is now tight and angry.

"But it could give you ideas about what set him off. You said you'll check on him tomorrow. What else can we do? He did talk about some of his *issues* the other night, but you know him much better than me."

Rory sighs. "Fair enough. But sometimes I just wonder what you *feel* and think about, besides those paintings. Maybe that's why I'm not a successful artist . . . because I want a *life*. You're so single-minded. But for all your faults you're still doing creative things, while too many people I used to know are frustrated with boring jobs or gone mad on too many drugs."

"Like Jonny?"

"Jonny will be OK," Rory insists again. "I know he will. But show me this man in the woods. Maybe it'll take my mind off things. You're right, lots of worrying won't help."

"I'm painting him, and some of his friends. You can help. You helped me with that other section, didn't you?" I start to undo my dressing gown.

"Helen, you really don't need to do that!"

"I like it this way. I'm freer to move, and I feel closer to the work."

"I'll keep my clothes on, thanks very much."

"Suit yourself. But tell me what you think of the painting. You work in three dimensions, so that gives you a different angle. I've been thinking again about perspective and the vanishing point. Maybe the place past the vanishing point is where 'the man in the woods' lives, and it's where I want to go. But there should be many ways to get there. And is it possible to show points where things *appear*?"

I lead him to another part I've been working on: the hillside near the Roman column where I had lain with Rachel. There's the pond where we washed ourselves. Within the pond I hint at shapes, starting with our reflection but transforming. "See there? How do I find a form that's more specific, but still fluid? Some say I should leave more to the imagination. But too often that's a cop-out."

I dab green and yellow in, thread in white. I suggest rays of sun breaking through foliage onto the water. Beneath the surface is a shape that is partly me and partly Rachel, and also a sprite-to-be.

Rory puts his fingers straight into the paint, giving it more form. "Problem with you painters, you *are* distant from your work if you're always at the other end of brush—clothes on or off. You need to put in more of yourself, do some finger-painting and get your hands dirty."

So I dab paint on with my fingertip, then get bolder. He's right. Handling the paint helps me feel the rounded shapes, the wet shapes.

As we're working I glance at Rory, who is looking under the weather. All the worry about his friend isn't doing him good. Sometimes, I wonder what it's like to care so much about someone. Perhaps I once cared about Rachel, but it was so long ago.

Rory might have had red hair before it went grey, but it would have been a light orange-red rather than Rachel's auburn. There are still strands of ginger glinting in his stubble. No, I don't go for stubble or whiskers. It's smooth skin that I crave. Or there could be down, neither feathers nor fur. I like glossy leaves or springy grass against me. Hair cascading over bare shoulders and legs. Long fingers, a probing tongue. Full breasts, lithe arms with taut muscles. Hot breath that blows over us, bringing summer with it. Water that carries us and fills us.

This is what our hands shape in the paint as we move from the pond to the rest of the scene. Our fingers touch. He is too absorbed to notice what is starting to happen.

"Shall we put *her* in this section, next to him? Close, as if they are almost the same entity . . . then becoming more distinct."

"This is a painting, not a film. It's only a static image," says Rory.

"But the image can spur something in a viewer's mind that isn't static. Like this . . . " I begin painting in the Panisca. I saw the way Rory looked at her, drawn to the warmth and compassion in her gaze. I cannot offer him that. Perhaps the figure we create will, though there's no compassion in the landscape she inhabits.

We correct each other's mistakes, add to each other's triumphs. I caress the Panisca's breasts as I add shadow. When I touch Rory's skin, it's smoother, the colour deepening. His muscles move under my fingers as if reaching, stretching towards a code that will unlock and lengthen them.

The change slides over my own skin like water, a liquid layer stirred by so many tongues, so many hands. I can think and become. My flesh and bones are pliant, and much more powerful. When I speak, my voice is high and ringing. I have grown younger, yet my origins are much more ancient.

In this space between the places the forest is dark but you step into the light on the cliffs. The mountain air smells of thyme and wild roses clinging to life in stony soil.

"Is it you, Helen? What *are* you?"

Rachel had looked at me this way when my companion first met us from the sky, or when I wrapped her in sinewy vines. I've also seen this on Meyrick's face, in Jonny's eyes. But there is also wonder, there is also desire.

"I am still Helen, but Helen can take many forms. And who do you want to be? What do you want to see? Don't tell me. Think of it and be it."

I lift my breast in my hands, offering it. "You admired the girl in the statue. I saw how you looked at her. A long time ago she lived, now I've taken her form, for I can be *everything*. And who are you now? When you change, it's like watching a reflection in a pond after you throw a stone. It breaks up, and comes together again."

As he bends towards me, more changes sweep over him. His hair turns dark. It is thick against my chest, dry from the sun, still holding that heat in it.

This way of changing is like a dance. You touch, you move, the other reacts. Then your partner makes a move and grows in an unforeseen way. The dance spirals from there.

"Rory, you said I wasn't your type, but now I am—much more than you ever thought."

At the end of it, the place is in a shambles. Paints and bottles lie smeared and shattered. Feathers and petals from exotic flowers are stuck to the ceiling. Fur belonging to no known animal is scattered in clumps on the floor, sticking to furniture and Rory's ripped clothes.

When I clean up I'll put these remnants in a trunk where they'll be safe. But for now, I just relish the afterglow, the vitality. This is what unlocks me from that single, stolid form. It makes me what I am. This is what lets me live for a long, long time.

Rory lies back, stunned but rather pleased with himself. "Helen, that was . . . awesome." Then he throws back his head and laughs. Hearty laughs that keep coming, until they crescendo out of control.

Once he calms down, I'll explain everything. And I'll tell him who his father is.

Rory stops laughing. "Didn't you ever get into trouble for doing shit like this?"

XI
THE LADY VANISHES

OF COURSE I GOT INTO TROUBLE. After Rachel left, there was an almighty row in the village.

The police questioned me: "You were her friend. Surely you know where she went? What did you talk about when you were together? And where were you the afternoon Rachel went missing?"

I'd been in my room at the Ross's, looking at the Pan and Panisca statue she'd given me, wondering if I should try to speak to her again. Mrs Ross had knocked on my door to offer me tea.

I told the police what would make sense to them. And what could they prove?

Nothing, of course. But still, the Rosses declined to be my hosts any longer.

Dr Raymond did not meet me at the station on my return. He did not greet me at the door. I went to him. He was in his library, hunched over a pile of books.

"I'm back," I announced, though I knew he didn't care.

"So you are."

"It wasn't my fault. The police interviewed me, I told the truth. She was unhappy, she must have run away. Maybe she went to London. They let me be because I did nothing wrong.

I was a friend to Rachel, and she was a friend to me. We had an argument, as girls often do."

He turned around, and I was shocked at the change in him. His grey hair had turned white. His scalp showed through with the texture of parchment. A multitude of new lines covered his face, and one eye was reddened and weeping.

"If you did nothing wrong, why did Ross send you back? I even offered to increase your money, but he wouldn't have you!"

"He was listening to rumours. He was afraid of me because I'm a little . . . different. They're just narrow-minded village snobs. No wonder Rachel went away! She was an intelligent girl, too smart for the likes of them."

"So you do know where Rachel is."

"No, I don't! We had an argument, and she stopped speaking to me. But if you don't believe me you can get an account from the police. I told them everything."

Then I exploded, sick of it all. "What is wrong with you? You behave as if you want nothing to do with me, yet you treat me as your possession. Why was I here in the first place, and why do you send me away? I keep asking you, but you've never told me anything."

"You know why I sent you away. It was that thing you were playing with. Not once, but several times, I saw you with him. With *it*."

"So." I crossed my arms and regarded him. "Is that all? And aren't you curious? That's why you subjected me to those examinations. Isn't that why you kept me in the first place? Now, I can tell you fascinating things. Why bury yourself in your books and laboratory when something extraordinary is here at hand and I can introduce you to it? You pestered me with questions when I was just a child trying to sleep. Now you refuse to listen."

"Yes, once I believed I could study you and ensure the tragedy hadn't been in vain. But it's because of my curiosity that terrible things have happened. What I saw when . . . "

"What did you see? Tell me!"

He sighed and shook his head. "I only saw its effects on your mother. Poor Mary . . . She was a loving girl who never meant harm. While you . . . even when you were a babe in the cradle, I looked into your eyes and saw *nothing*. But Mary still loved you with whatever strength she had left. In one of her few lucid moments she asked me to look after you.

"So she did *not* die giving birth to me. You lied!"

"Did I ever say she died in childbirth? You assumed that, but the truth is far worse. The horror started with your very *conception*, yet Mary only regarded you as a child in need of care. I'll continue to keep my promise to her though you make my skin crawl. You look so much like your mother, but you lack her most vital attribute—a soul."

"And what about my mother? For years you've been saying you're sorry. So what did you do to her? Did you violate her, take advantage of her trust? The worst I could ever imagine is that *you* are my father. Anything is better. All your *sorries* . . . well, you will be sorry when I . . . "

"Are you threatening me? Do I have to fetch the police here like that poor girl's parents had to do? But you won't be here long. I found a school for you and you leave tomorrow."

I was restless when I went to sleep in my old bedroom. All my girlish things were there. That damned rocking horse. The trunk of dolls and toys. A sampler that had never been sewn.

As I surveyed the clutter of the life meant to be mine, I felt only desolation.

Rachel must have felt the same in her village, wherever she could be now.

Would it be London? Or Paris, or further? Did she go searching for *him*? I'll look for her. Or I'll go *somewhere*. Soon. Rachel was right when she said there was more to life than playing in the woods.

With my resolution to travel taking shape, I drifted into visions of leaving the rainswept hills behind and stretching out in the sun again, far from this room in a crumbling, cold house. Because I felt so alone, I began to sing to myself. I tried to form the melodies he played on his pipe, the songs that vibrated in the trembling air and restless earth when he was near. I smelled fresh trampled grass and tasted fruit on my tongue.

And then, *he* was with me again. He was stuffed into his more usual man-shape, golden-skinned and golden-eyed.

"Where have you been? Don't leave me again."

"I will never leave you. I never have."

"It's been months."

"Months? When you mature you'll lose the habit of measuring time."

"But who are you, and who am I?"

"I know little more than you," he said. "I found myself lost, and caught between . . . worlds. That is why I must touch everything. It is to anchor myself here, yet ease my transition to the other places. It will help me find my way back to where I come from."

His voice was deep and dripping with music.

I was still Helen, but I was long and laden with fruit that was red and sweet. I reached for his music and felt my fruits ripen, skins split with abundance. As he licked the juice, the point of his tongue stretched me to the point of unmaking.

"This is who you are. Unfixed, a form that is all things, the form of all life and your life."

Unmade, I was remade.

The next day I went to the selected boarding school. I didn't oppose it. I was relieved. My step was sprightly as I climbed onto my train. I was back in my usual shape, but being with him had transformed me in my mind, and the vitality of my body.

The horror started with your very conception.

That filthy old man. I was glad to be going far away from him.

The school? It was much the same as the last one. Again, I found places to visit in the woods. The headmistress followed Dr Raymond's instructions and gave me my own room.

This time I attended lessons, though the educational fare for "young ladies" was limited. But I took what I could from it. I wanted to learn about the world Rachel had spoken about, one full of libraries and theatres and learned debates. I was almost eighteen and I knew I had to make my way in the world, preferably somewhere far from where I grew up.

So I became a good pupil. And when I went into the forest, no one said anything as long as I dressed suitably and protected my complexion from the elements.

My companion had resumed his visits, especially when I learned ways to get his attention. Summoning him wasn't like calling a cab. I needed to tempt him. He loved little rituals and signs and jokes. I could lie upon the grass and spread my arms and legs to embrace the earth. I could lift my hand and make a fluid motion, or begin a particular dance.

And, of course, I learned to sing more of his songs. Though I couldn't create the same sounds, I began to understand the power of music and voice.

A few notes of a favourite song drew him quickest of all.

"So now you come to me when I call," I said to him. "Why did you stop?" It was a question I asked from time to time. He was always patient in his answers.

"I lose track of your time. But now, your voice is louder. I hear you more often."

"So where is this place you talk about, the place you come from? Take me there."

"I'm still looking for it. And I can't take you there because you're also a part of this world, and a part of you will always want to stay in it too. We are not the same."

"Who *is* like me then?"

His only answer to that question was a slow sad tune on his pipes.

So many years later I still think of what my companion said: *We are not the same.* At the time it meant that *he* didn't have to go to school. He came and went as he pleased.

Yes, it's true we are not all the same. And we are not easy to find. It is something I must feel with my skin. I can't tell just by looking or speaking to someone.

During my first sojourn in London I regularly consulted a clairvoyant based at Paul Street in Soho. I told her I was looking for lost relations. I didn't say what kind. In the end, she was little help to me.

At the beginning of the last century I accidentally brushed against a man on the street. It was a warm day, but he was clothed in a long coat. He also wore a hat and gloves. But as he reached out to hail a cab his sleeve pulled back to bare his lower arm as it brushed against me. I felt the difference, a thrill of recognition and a drive to connect. Questions crowded my mind, and I wanted to shout them at once to him. I grabbed his arm.

He turned towards me. Both longing and loathing filled his golden-brown eyes, which widened at our contact. His beard was also golden-brown, and it began to feel like fur when I reached out to touch it.

Then a cab stopped for him. He shook me off, opened the door and fell inside, slamming it after him.

XII
THE EXPERIMENT

TIME PASSED AT THE SCHOOL, my last school. But of course, things change.

A letter arrived for me. For a moment, I had hopes it would be from Rachel.

But it came from Dr Raymond's solicitor, writing that the doctor had died and I must return to the house and settle his affairs. Estranged from his family, he had named me as beneficiary and executor of his estate. Though he had loathed me, he left me everything.

This must be part of his promise to "poor Mary", his reparation. But what did he do to her?

I met the keen gaze of the headmistress, who had handed me the letter. "Well, Helen? What is it?"

I told her Dr Raymond had died and I must leave. I didn't know when I would return.

She didn't seem sorry to hear that I might leave for good, though I'd been behaving myself. Perhaps it was because I didn't cry for Dr Raymond.

When I arrived at the house I found the furniture and curtains coated with dust. The cook and the maid were preparing to leave and only waited for me to arrive so I could pay their last wages. I went through his desk and found piles of cash, equally dust coated. After payment, the servants slipped away, leaving me in the house with the old man's remains.

I discovered food in the pantry, which tasted of the must that pervaded the house. Then I walked through the corridors and every room. Everywhere were pictures of my mother.

I arranged for the undertaker to remove the corpse, but set no date for a funeral. I only instructed him to bury the man in the appropriate place and be done. Dr Raymond's coffin had been closed when I arrived, and closed it stayed.

But I later delved into his papers with eagerness. I wasn't sure what I was looking for. Then I found it: a file with my name. *Helen Vaughan.*

He had arranged the items in the folder by date and subject. Here, a series of measurements: "Helen at birth". Length. Circumference of head. Five fingers on each hand, five toes on each foot: "fully formed, no webbing, hooves or malformations". My mouth became drier than the dust rising from the box. "Genitalia: normal."

There were notes, scraps from my bedside interviews. "Leaves like hands. Tickled. Delusional? Perverse."

I picked up a little sealed box. I shook it. Hard things rattled inside. Not jewels, surely. I prised off the lid with a letter opener. Inside, a number of bumpy objects, yellowed brown and white. Teeth. I dropped the box and they scattered over the desktop. So tiny—they must be my milk teeth. With a swipe of my arm I sent the teeth rolling and skipping off the desk.

More notes. "Eyes: abnormally dark brown, almost black." *Abnormal?* I looked at yet another picture of my mother, whose eyes could have been grey or blue. She must have been about my age. She wore a plain dress with a high collar that made me put my hand to my throat in discomfort. But those light eyes regarded the world with a gleam of wonder. It made me think of what flooded through me when I played in the woods with my companion, and with Rachel. Or the night I spent here on my last visit. The touch of my companion's tongue, those moments of unmaking and becoming.

What had Mary been looking for when she sat for that picture? What was she seeing when she was driven mad?

I found another box labelled "Mary Vaughan". Could it contain the answer?

In Mary's box was a folder too: "The Experiment". I began to read.

As I paint, I move forward and back in time, from one panel to another. Do I want to show the laboratory and study? It would be painted in dingy browns and tired whites, not the colours I enjoy working with. But it's part of the story.

I remember the rattle of my milk teeth in that box.

Here it is, Dr Raymond's window looking over the meadows, the fields and orchards. The desk, a trail of teeth that lead out the window. I paint each tooth with precision. They were already yellow and brown with age when I found them. But I make them white and new as they were when I hid them under my pillow, just as Cerys had once instructed.

Dr Raymond had written: "I see the mountains, the woods and orchards and meadows. It tempts me away from my studies. There is stillness in the heat of a summer day, yet it is full of movement. There is the hum of bees and unknown insects, the cries of animals."

I was surprised that he loved the countryside as I did. Didn't he scold me for playing in the woods? Other passages in his notebooks echoed my own overwhelming need to know, a lust in its own right. I only had different ways of trying to find things out.

I dot more teeth in a trail out the window, through the fields and into the woods until they can't be seen. But they're still there. How do I show that?

The trail of baby teeth goes into the woods. Do they lead to another thicket or dark grove, or across the field where Rachel was last seen? Maybe the trail of teeth should lead *out* of the past. Into his world, past the vanishing point.

I'm stuck. I stop painting, clean my hands and switch on the computer.

My inbox is full of emails about the last open house. One less-than-complimentary message makes me pause:

> Dear Ms Vaughan,
>
> You may recall that I purchased a painting from you with the title of *Sprites*. At my daughter's request I displayed it in my home before installing it in my gallery.
>
> However, Natasha has recently displayed erratic behaviour. She has moved the painting to her room and locks herself in with it. She has shunned her friends and entertains an array of inappropriate guests. She has been over-eating and has put on at least a stone.
>
> I've decided to contact you after an incident of her disturbed behaviour at a public exhibition. While I know that a work of art is not like a faulty piece of equipment I can return for a refund, I urge that you carefully consider the impact of your work in the future.
>
> *Sprites* has been removed from my home and is now in storage. If you are unhappy with the situation, I am open to negotiations if you wish to buy the painting back.
>
> Sincerely,
> Franklin Forbes

My first response is enraged deletion, and a plan to rescue my painting. Then I recover the email. I think about a response. I don't know why Natasha and Jonny react the way they do. Or why all those gentlemen keeled over some time ago. Or why I was sacked from a position as a receptionist because they thought I was "frightening" the customers. I don't mean anyone harm. That's what Dr Raymond said about my mother, and the same is true about me. I don't mean harm. I'm just being myself.

I still don't know exactly what that means. But I knew even less the day I went through Dr Raymond's papers.

"I rescued Mary from the gutter and she is mine to use," Dr Raymond had written.

There was barely enough light to see as the afternoon began to fade. But I read on.

He wrote of mysterious nerves in the brain called into activity by a "touch", which would let Mary see beyond the veil to the "spirit world".

You were wrong, dear doctor, for the world you sought has much more than "spirit" to offer. It is full of flesh: it bursts with it.

I extended my arm, drew my fingernail along it.

This is real, I thought. This is skin and bone. I am real. So is my companion. I touched the side of my own head. Was it simply a few nerves there that made me so different?

I let the papers fall to the floor as I imagined Dr Raymond in a bloody smock waiting for my mother to awaken. Mary opens her eyes and looks around, face flooded with her illumination. Then she shrieks in terror and turns into a "mindless idiot".

Mary has seen the "Great God Pan".

Nine months later, she has a child—me.

I paced about the room. It didn't make sense. Mary stayed in her bed, nursed and watched by Dr Raymond and his staff. No fun in the forest for her.

Dr Raymond had reported no ravishment. Had he been too prudish to refer to it directly? Or was my conception his work after all?

Then I remembered the old song.

> So the lady ran into her chamber,
> And she changed into a bed,
> Ah, but he became a green coverlet,
> And he gained her maidenhead.

This time my companion came quickly when I called for him.

"So why didn't you tell me? What did you do to her?"

"What was there to tell? You knew these things all along," he replied.

"Not entirely. Not clearly. I even thought *Dr Raymond* was my father. But it's you!"

Should it matter that my companion had fathered me and he was also my lover?

I felt only relief. Much better to be related to *him* than to Dr Raymond. It explained things I should have seen, but ignored in an all-too-human way.

As soon as it became clear what kind of conversation we were having, he made himself ordinary: a larger and more handsome man, hair not combed in the day's fashion and his usual bit of greenery stuck in it. But essentially, he appeared to be a man.

"What is a father? What is a mother?" He interrupted his rhetorical questions with a sigh. "Do those things matter with *us*? Yes, it could have been me, or any of the others who come with me. It could have been a sprite, a speck of dust or dew on a blade of grass. You are partly a child of my entire world. Life gives birth to life, and like calls to like. That's why I'm here, and you are who you are."

"So how did you—or whoever it was—get my mother pregnant? Turn into a coverlet, like the song says? Did you force her?"

My companion's reply was only laughter, a special thing. His laughter bubbled from deep from within him until it floated on the air. The trees and leaves shook with it; wind and water conspired with its mockery.

Then he added: "Helen, have I ever harmed you? Perhaps you listen to the wrong songs." He began playing one of his own songs and we danced.

"Who can say if a song is right or wrong," I ask, whirling to the pipes. "I have a new verse!" His pipes took up the melody as I sang:

> So the lady turned into a man,
> Moved upon him good,
> So he became a luscious wench,
> And she took him where he stood.

As the excitement seized me in the dance, I let my bones lengthen and felt a male member sprout between my legs. He reached over to stroke it and I changed more.

I could only do it when I was with him, stricken with music and desire. There's a crawling sensation as nerves grow and spread and others retract. It can itch, but that only makes scratching the itch more pleasurable. I spread my palms over my chest as it grew flat and broad.

His hair lengthened and turned auburn, his skin became so fair. And I cried out, "No! Don't try to look like Rachel."

But it was only for a moment. Then the red hair darkened, and he became a plump brown-eyed maiden smelling of musk and spice.

Dr Raymond had left me with substantial funds as well as the house and grounds.

I put the crumbling property in care of an agent to sell. Then I booked a place on a ship bound for America. Rachel had mentioned America as a possible destination, and I thought it would appeal to her for the same reason it drew me. It was the furthest away.

Like Rachel, I wanted to see the world. And like Dr Raymond, I wanted to *know* and understand. I needed to experiment too.

When I had most of my things packed, I went to the laboratory and collected Dr Raymond's notes. Then I picked up a portrait of my mother. Shall I take it with me?

I gave it a long look. Dr Raymond had regarded her as a saint and angel—a fallen one—but an angel nonetheless.

No, she was just a woman. I held the portrait at arm's length. "Mary, what did you see? Was it *him*? He has never done me any harm. The worst is that he can be forgetful. But what frightened you so much?"

In this portrait, Mary's eyes were downcast and she wore the expression of a dog waiting for a whipping. *Will you stop that cringing!* I gave the picture a shake, as if I could be shaking the woman herself.

Why didn't you see what Dr Raymond was doing? Why did you submit?

I threw the portrait down in disgust. The broken glass crunched under my shoes as I fled from that room. I haven't been there since.

I believe that house is now managed by the Welsh Tourist Board, which rents it as a centre for business conferences and team-building games.

I wandered back and forth across the American continent. I didn't find Rachel. I didn't find any other answers. I headed south and ended up in Argentina. My companion followed.

In Buenos Aires I fell in with a colony of expatriates and drifters drawn by the easier living. Some were petty nobles, living the high life on the proceeds of declining estates. There were artists and refugees, adventurers and crooks. I felt at home. Though my education in upper-crust sin-bins had been limited, I learned fast and established myself at the centre of the expatriate salons. Meanwhile, I explored haunts that more fastidious foreigners feared to investigate—dives with dirt floors in the dusty barrios, festivities of natives who lived in the hinterlands.

Among the expatriates I met a young artist, Arthur Meyrick, whose curiosity also extended beyond the high society of Buenos Aires. I initiated him into my world, which he passionately embraced. While a familiar revulsion sometimes flickered across his face at the height of a revelation, he pursued it to its end.

Meyrick's eyes were almost as dark as mine. His background differed from that of the other expats; he was a self-educated man from the East End who had attracted the backing of a wealthy patron. There was something slightly foreign about him, which excited an odd sense of kinship. My companion took an interest in him too.

What would you have us be? I asked. Meyrick wasn't always able to tell us, but we always found out.

Afterwards, Meyrick would draw. Sometimes I told stories of my past and expressed my imaginings. Or my companion played his music and Meyrick created pictures from that.

The fauns danced, the sprites and agile nymphs cavorted. There were dark thickets and waterweeds, whirligigs on craggy mountaintops, revels on deserted shores, in vineyards, within circles of stones and feral forests. They invoked longing for something that had been a part of me, a place I've never seen. Dr Raymond's crude surgery, his small "rearrangement of cells", had left so much out. *Poor Mary.*

I looked at the drawings, beginning to understand. I had told my tales, but as soon as words were uttered, the stories were gone. Writing them down did not appeal to me. But Meyrick was able to turn words into something you could look at and touch, again and again.

"Arthur, will you teach me how to draw?"

"I don't think art can be taught," Meyrick said stiffly. "But I can show you the basics." He talked me through some sketches.

By then I was accustomed to shifts in my physical self, but this was the first time I felt something move and alter within. My attention condensed to the point of contact of the pen between my fingers, the soft hiss of it against the paper. And when Meyrick explained perspective and the vanishing point, something fell in place.

Meyrick thought it was a matter of how you drew lines, and their angle to one another. But I had learned at an early age to look past what was visible. Could the vanishing point be where my companion comes from? Perhaps it is more than a simple point, but a whole other world of colour and movement.

My first strokes with the charcoal were careful and considered; next thing my charcoal flew every which way over the paper.

Meyrick wasn't impressed with the results. "Looks like a bloody mess," he said.

XIII
LOOSE CANNON

"DON'T BE SO MISERABLE, RORY. You remind me of Meyrick, this guy I knocked about with in Buenos Aires. He got gloomy because he couldn't do what *we* can do. And you . . . " I throw up my hands. "Or is it Jonny? Are you worried about him?"

Rory slumps forward, chin resting on his hand and his eyes focused on a puddle of beer on the table. "No. It's not Jonny. Jonny is a lot better."

This is the first time I've seen Rory since our transformative encounter. I'm now taking him out for a drink at the Belfry and then a gig downstairs, a band he's been keen to see.

When I revealed what we have in common, Rory took it surprisingly well and didn't even try to explain it all away as a bad acid trip. But now he looks about to plunge into his pint of Shoreditch Stout.

Yet, aside from his downcast expression, Rory is looking good. His skin is smoother in a way that suggests something other than a good close shave. It's firmer, more moist. Is there a touch more ginger than grey in his hair now? The difference is subtle, but in view of what I know, unmistakeable.

I reach over and give him a prod. "Rory, have you had a look in the mirror recently? Did you notice you're a little more fresh-faced? The transformations affect ageing."

"But I've already aged a lot. And we've got to shag each other for it to work, don't we?"

"Is that so bad? You seemed to enjoy it at the time. And don't tell me I'm not your type. You're not my type either. But that's something easily remedied, given our abilities."

"You mean, we can *change*? But that's fake. Maybe I was taken in when you first turned into that Pan-girl. But it was you underneath. She looks like a creature who *gives*. And you . . . "

"Yes, I know what I'm like. But what about you? Maybe the changing *can* make you youthful again. I don't know for certain, because I started when I was still young."

"You had someone to show you. But our fucker of a father didn't want to know in my case."

"But that *fucker's* not here now for me, is he? But with two of us . . . it can be different."

"Yeah, I'm up for trying," says Rory. "I want to get hold of the bastard and give him a piece of my mind. And I'd like to know how many other by-blows of his are running about!"

"You're the only 'by-blow' I've *spoken* to. As for others . . . I missed one in a crowd over a century ago; another had no control over the changes and was confined in an asylum."

"Lovely. So what did you do to get your *friend* to come to you?"

"It used to be easy. But I think he's further away now. He's trying to go 'home'."

"What, thinks he's ET does he? What bollocks," Rory grumbles. "My fucking father. Sorry if I've been a pain, but I feel like crap. Like a comedown after a shit acid trip. And now I've found out you're my sister of sorts—my half-sister—it's put me off. No offence, but . . . "

I put up my hand to ward off further apologies. "Rory, I'm sure we'll find a way around it. But most people would be *thrilled*, and with you it's one complaint after another . . . "

He becomes even more morose. "You know, unlike a lot of adopted children, I didn't get upset when I couldn't find anything about my birth parents. They weren't in my life, and I had a good family who was. But now that's changed. I keep wondering about my mum."

I decide not to tell him what happened to *my* mum.

"I realise this is difficult to adjust to, but try to be positive . . . Think of the things you can do." I'm a bit stuck. Being comforting and supportive isn't usually part of my repertoire. "I'm sorry I can't give you many answers, but I'm always here . . . " I reach across the table again and pat him on his shoulder.

"Don't touch me." He pushes me away. "I mean, the last thing I want to do is turn into a . . . a whatever . . . in the middle of the pub."

"Calm down, it's not like that. A full-on change doesn't happen any time we touch. Whatever gives us our ability to transform only works when we concentrate and desire it. So it *won't* happen in the middle of the pub unless you want it to."

"I still don't understand how it happens though. And how are we different?"

"I'm only guessing, but it might be something at a cellular level, perhaps a capacity that works like embryonic stem cells," I suggest. "They can grow into anything, can't they? Or it's how elements behave on different planes, and our makeup has imported these properties. But no one knows. I'm not about to cut myself up and look at my bits under a microscope. I'm not a scientist. I *hate* scientists."

"What?" Rory is startled. "What do you have against scientists? It's only something people do for a job. One of the guys I used to travel with went back to university and studied physics. Seemed a nice enough bloke. He used to do more drugs than me and Jonny together. Maybe I'll have a word about . . . "

"No, no, you don't want to do that. He'll just think you're mad."

Rory snorts. "But you know who I really do want to talk to? I want to meet that *bastard*!" He hits the table with his fist, setting our glasses shaking.

"You must understand that *he* doesn't keep track of time in the same way," I say. "He moves about in places where time is different. Everything is different. The things we think are important don't count over there. And he has his sights set elsewhere."

"Bollocks, that's the biggest load of bollocks yet. I don't care where he is, it's no excuse for this *being* to be irresponsible and not give a fuck. How many people like us has he left wandering about? He owes us an explanation, at least."

"So, at least we both want to bring him here. Things I used to do . . . are not enough now. That's what the paintings are for. And the gatherings, the open house."

"Huh? I don't get it. So there was weird stuff going on last time. But I've been to weird parties before. What was different about that one? I had to leave early . . . " Rory rubs his nose. "That *stuff* really did me in. But I'll take my antihistamines next time . . . "

I interrupt him. "Rory, it *was* different. You sniffed the evidence, though I'm sorry it didn't agree with you. Something came through . . . "

"But it wasn't our man with the pipes, was it? I don't know. But you can still count me in. I'm willing to try, 'cause I want words with this so-called father of ours."

"He doesn't mind antagonism. In fact he thrives on it. I do too, sometimes."

"Don't I know that. Oh come on, Hel, let's go downstairs. Maybe it'll cheer me up."

We go down, following the music and voices.

"Tell me about this geezer in Argentina," says Rory. "It sounds like you were close, or as close as you ever get to anyone."

"Meyrick gave me my first art lessons, but said my efforts looked like a 'bloody mess'."

"Sounds like a wanker, Hel. He obviously didn't know what he was talking about."

"Maybe, but he was a talented wanker. We didn't part on good terms though. He said I'll never be an artist: I'm just a spoiled brat with a few oddities. So my feelings for him changed. And my companion began to treat him with scorn too. He once changed entirely to a goat and ate several of Meyrick's drawings. He munched his shoes for dessert."

"No way!" Rory bursts out with a good rude laugh and I join in. I don't think I ever talked about those times to *anyone*. It gives me an unexpected rush of pleasure.

The gig is in the exhibit room, now set up with a makeshift bar in the corner where we wait to get another round of drinks. I nod at familiar faces. And one of them nods back at me in an overly enthusiastic way, as if trying to convince himself that everything is OK.

It's Jonny, without the dreads. He nods again and surprises me by smiling.

"Alright Jonny?" I greet him. "I'm glad to see that you're out and about and feeling better. Rory's here. Care to join us?"

I buy another pint for him, and point towards a few seats that are still empty.

"Don't mind if I do. Long as we're not looking at your painting," he says with a chuckle. "That was just too intense."

I raise my glass to him, knowing he's talking about more than my paintings.

Meanwhile, the band gets on stage and starts tuning. Then the accordion player lets out a raucous cackle as the band strikes up in a fury of guitars, fiddles and bodhráns. She begins singing and whooping about "whiskey or death" and "cider and smithereens". Another song recounts a barney at the dole office.

Rory is staring gape-mouthed at the singer. I see why, for she's a fine figure of a woman. She's a good six feet tall, with a mass of kinky pale hair falling over broad shoulders and cleavage as deep as her shoulders are wide. Hefty arms make that squeeze box cry out for mercy amid the sweetness of its tunes. Her long skirt clings over muscular legs and a bountiful bottom. Her large-featured face could have been sculpted from the side of a mountain, yet it's full of emotion and movement.

Jonny also appears suitably awestruck.

At the end of the song she introduces herself as Mandy and the band as Bag O' Shite.

"Do you like her?" I ask Rory. "She's definitely your type. Do you want to meet her?"

"Why? Do you know her?"

"No, but I will if I want to. And if you do too."

"No, Helen, you'll embarrass me."

"I've done far worse than embarrass people."

Mandy gets the squeeze box going again. All this brings a bit of colour to Jonny's cheeks and soon he's tapping a spoon against the arm of his chair.

"This is a traditional song, but it could be about my old flatmates," Mandy says, and she starts singing about the bonny mad boys of Bedlam:

118

For they all go bare, and they live by the air,
And they want no drink nor money . . .

My own sight of Bedlam was not so "bonny": a relation of mine quivering on the floor, caught between shapes so as to become shapeless. I had to bribe the keeper to see this. Perhaps Mr Machen did too, and that's where he found the idea for the death he had fashioned for me in his story.

Folks are singing now and shouting along; some get out of their seats and dance. Jonny is knocking the back of a chair with his empty beer glass along with the song. I see the cuts under the stubble of his shaved head, and a wildness to his glass-banging as he shouts. "Bonny mad boys! I'm a bonny mad boy!" A few drops arc out of Jonny's glass and the guy in front turns around to glare, then pulls his chair further away.

At the finish of "Bedlam Boys" Mandy announces another traditional song. "This one's known to be even dodgier than the last," she says. "But I'll sing it with a *happy* ending!" And then she strikes up some very familiar chords.

The lady sits at her own front door,
As straight as a willow wand,
And by there come a lusty smith,
With his hammer in his hand . . .

"Oooh, I like a man who can handle his hammer, with good form and all," chortles a young lad with pink hair.

"No matter what form he takes!" I add.

Though I don't shout, I know how to make my voice heard. Mandy turns and meets my eyes as she lets sighs of melody float from her accordion. "You know the song then?"

"Yes, it's one of my favourites."

Perhaps something in my voice alerted Mandy to its capabilities, for she invites me up to sing with her. I beam at everyone as I join her. "So how about if I sing the blacksmith and you can be the lady?"

Mandy nods at my suggestion. She has large tawny eyes that make me think of a tigress, albeit a drunken and amiable one that would purr if you scratched her the right way behind the ears. She sings:

> *So the lady took out her wand, waved it high into the air,*
> *And she turned into a cloud, saying "Catch me if you dare."*

This is a different version than the one I learned, but still I know an answer:

> *So the blacksmith swung his hammer,*
> *And it turned into a magic stick,*
> *So he became a lightning bolt,*
> *And he zapped into her quick.*

Mandy's gritty voice rings with a new clarity. "*So the lady she turned into a fiddle, hid amidst a song . . .*"

I come back with: "*And he became a bow and he played her all night long.*"

My voice changes too as I assume my role. Though Mandy is by far brawnier, I now feel as if I'm the big man with the hammer. I'm the "coal-black smith". I'm the dark one who stokes the fire and wields the power to change the shape of steel.

A terrified shriek comes from the audience.

"The man in the woods! The man in the woods!"

It's Jonny, standing and pointing at me. "The man in the woods!"

"C'mon, Jonny. It's only Helen." Rory gently ushers his friend out, with a nod to me.

"*The man in the woods!*" still echoes from the corridor.

Taking up the cue, Mandy sings *"And* she *became a man, a dark man in the wood . . . "*

She plays a few rounds of melody on the accordion to give me time to think.

And what would happen if all the woods were gone? So I sing:

> *And he became a JCB,*
> *That took the woods away . . .*

Amid the laughter greeting this verse, Mandy brings us back to the old finale where the lady turns into a bed. I sing the standard response.

> *But he became a green coverlet,*
> *And he gained her maidenhead.*

Mandy grins, playing the accordion softly as she speaks above it to the audience. She draws closer to me.

"That's usually the last verse," she explains. "But in my version it's the lady who has the last word . . . that's if our lovely blacksmith here don't mind!"

"Of course not." I put my arm around her. "There's always another verse to this song."

"We'll see about that!" Then Mandy sings:

> *For she became a spider,*
> *When the blacksmith became her mate,*

And though he gained her maidenhead,
The blacksmith then she ate,

Crying, "Bide, blacksmith, bide,
There's nowhere you can hide,
For though you gained my maidenhead,
I've got you now inside."

Our friendly argument continues on the way to my place after the gig. "No, Mandy, it doesn't have to end just because you eat the blacksmith!"

"It does! It does!"

"Let me ask this—did you swallow him whole? He can change to something else. Or maybe he can change to a female spider just when you're about to eat him. And the two girl spiders go for it! Didn't think about that, did you?"

"Maybe not. Maybe we should do that song again. We made a good double act. But do you think that guy will be OK? The one who was shouting?"

"That's Jonny. He's had some trouble, mental health trouble. He overdid things in his raving days. My mate Rory's taken him home. By the way, Rory was very impressed with your band. He'd like to meet you."

"That big guy with you? I noticed him. He seemed so sweet and solid, the way he looked after his friend. And he had such a nice smile. I could tell he was really enjoying the music."

The lift clanks up to my floor, but I don't turn on the light straight away. Mandy clears her throat, as if she's having doubts.

"Stand here for the best view. I *did* invite you up to see my paintings," I assure her. "I'll put the light on now. Your songs gave me a feeling you'd find them of interest."

"It's funny, Helen. You have a posh way of talking, but there's something about you that isn't like that at all."

"You might say I've always been a loose cannon. I was sent to boarding schools, but I was also expelled from them."

"For what?"

"Oh, the usual. But you might see some of that story in this painting. You can think about the sections as chapters in a book called *Helen's Story*. This is *Where the Places Meet*. We can call this part *The Man in the Woods*, and that's *Vanishing Points* over there. Some don't have names yet, especially the smaller ones. They were just practice runs."

When I flip the switch the room is flooded with a pale light. Mandy's face goes pale too. Her tawny cat's eyes are wide, pupils like pinpricks as if she'd taken a drug.

"Shit! There really is a man in the woods."

XIV
WHAT FLAVIUS SAW

WHEN I SKETCH MYSELF I make my face more angular, as if I *am* the "man in the woods".

I begin drawing my mother too, a ghost at my shoulder. Will I show Mary as the young girl, or the broken woman with vacant eyes after a botched operation? Maybe I'll introduce her to the "man in the woods" as it should have been. Did she ever hear his music, did she ever dance to it?

Scrabbling and buzzing and metallic clicking interrupt my thoughts. The sounds come from the window.

I go to investigate. A beetle the size of my palm is trapped inside the double glazing. There's barely enough room for it to move between the two panes. It slaps its wings against both sides in a whirr of emerald and turquoise. When it rises within the glass, I see that its mid-section is feathered. Its mandibles must be sharp. They should be making marks upon the creature's prison. But the glass shows no signs of the beetle's struggles.

I want to get the insect out, but I'd have to take the window apart. By that time, it will be dead.

I can't work with that noise. Beating, buzzing.

A moment of silence. Then the buzz starts again on a higher register.

When the phone rings, it's a relief. I run to answer it.

It's only Nao again. She keeps phoning, and coming over too. She chatters, then looks long and hard at the paintings, drinking them in the way she drinks her Chardonnay.

"How are preparations for your thing, I mean, your show going?" Her normally crisp diction sounds fuzzy, as if she has the receiver covered with a sponge.

"Nao, I've told you, it's not a show . . . it's an open house and I've invited people to help finish the paintings. Lots of people are coming. But there's a fucking bug stuck in the middle of the window that's driving me crazy. It's stuck right in the middle of the double-glazing. I can hear it now."

"How'd it get there? But never mind, why don't you ask your . . . that handyman with the van to sort it out?"

"If you're talking about Rory, he's also busy getting work ready. He's bringing his stuff over today. Did I tell you that I invited him to take part?"

"D'you think that's a good idea? Maybe this open house is getting too *open*. Won't s-sho-ome drunk munter chuck his drink on the paintings?"

Nao's slurred words make me think of the old line about pots making certain remarks to kettles, but I don't mention that. "So what?" I reply. "Red wine will add colour."

But I do add that I'm a bit nervous.

"Bah! You, nervous?" There's the sound of liquid being poured. She doesn't say anything after that.

"Nao? You still there? You OK?" When there's no answer, I decide that she must have found something else to occupy her attention and I hang up.

I *am* getting anxious. This could be the first time in years I've assembled such a group. Can I inspire the movements, the right pitch of revelry to unravel the curtain between his world and mine? But what are the requirements now? The so-called goal posts have moved.

When I go back to the window, I see that the beetle has died. The sheen has left its wings, its body dried to a husk.

125

I feel a strange regret about that beetle. It's only a bug. But where did it come from? Where was it trying to go?

I don't want that dried-out dead thing to remain there. And I also want a closer look, as if it will help me understand.

I knock on the glass, trying to move the insect so I can see its mandibles, the feathered underside. My knocking becomes as frantic as the insect's unsuccessful bid to escape, but the vibration only jostles it slightly.

This business of the bug has broken my chain of thought. Rory and Mandy will be here soon. I return to the painting but I can't settle back with those portraits. I start to examine the Roman column in the foreground, another unfinished detail.

It's still smooth and featureless. "Flavius has erected this pillar on account of the marriage that he saw beneath the shade." That was on the original, but the image in front of me needs something else.

The smooth surface of my unfinished pillar reminds me of glass, the glass of my window. The bug made no marks on the window, but I can make them on the column. *This is how to get out.* My movements with the brush are sharp and staccato, then languid. They leave signs that have no reference to any language. They turn into curved impressions that could come from lips, a tongue, teeth. As I render the marks and tint them, they blend and move together, creating curves within curves. They are like the patterns I saw when I closed my eyes as I changed, a roadmap to an unknown country.

Scraping and banging from downstairs heralds the arrival of Rory and Mandy. Soon enough he comes in hefting a twisted piece of a car. Mandy follows, holding the other end of it. As usual she looks splendid in combat trousers that sit low on her broad hips, and a sleeveless t-shirt that shows off those arms.

126

"We've finally worked out how to move these things," says Mandy. "Simple really. Take 'em apart and put 'em together." She laughs, as if she's just told a joke. They both smile as they heft and lift, taking breaks to kiss and cuddle. The air in the flat shifts in the wake of their simple, sweaty human energy. Even the dust around the ill-fated insect stirs.

I help them move another mutated car seat in, then some trees. Real foliage mixed with the artificial gets in my eyes as Mandy and I wield one like a battering ram into the room. Rory brings in its base and we set it down to shade *Where the Places Meet*.

"Why don't you put on that pipe music again?" Mandy asks. "You gave me a copy, but it's not the same when I play it at home."

"Not again," Rory complains as he looks out the window. The light picks out the colour his hair has gained since our one shape-shifting session. But he still insists it's only *lurve* putting an extra spring in his step.

"Back by popular demand," I tell him. As my companion's music plays, we arrange the additions to the exhibit. Mandy whistles and then sings under her breath, though I don't get to hear her words.

Finally, there's only one more thing to move and place. When we put Rory's lavender-sprouting TV in a corner, I place the Panisca and her friends in the centre.

After Rory and Mandy leave, I survey the room. For all the time I've spent on these paintings, only now do I see them in relation to each other. Rory's trees and sculptures of twisted metal, fur and velvet offer further clues. Hopi had asked: "Where are the cities?" Rory has just added pieces of one.

Rory had also suggested I put more of myself into the work . . . so I will. I open up my trunk and dig out vines of dried ivy. The black leaves are now shiny and crisp; the vines, leathery. I drape them through the branches that hang over the paintings. I fashion bowers and tunnels that echo those on canvas, imparting a scent to the room between pine and a light animal musk.

I use gifts from my companion too—some were offered, others taken. Long feathers, curls of hair, parings from claws and talons.

Scales from a sprite add shimmer and texture to water-themed images.

And then there are more recent reminders left by Rory.

I turn on the lights as dusk settles. The trees and the ivy add shadow to Rachel's face as she stretches out in the sun on that hill. They shelter the pillar that Flavius had erected in honour of the marriage he saw beneath the shade.

So what did old Flavius see? I begin painting again as I try to see this too.

XV
BENEATH THE SHADE

WHILE MANDY STASHES HER ACCORDION in the bedroom cupboard, Rory stalks about the room. He whistles in admiration, he grins and blushes once or twice. "Y'know, our pieces do really complement each other. I wouldn't have thought that, given our disagreements. But if I had any doubts about this whole malarky . . . "

"Well, we have other things in common, don't we? Very important ones . . . "

"*Shhhsh!*" he hisses as Mandy joins us again. Then he makes another circuit around the room, giving a few tugs to the covering we'd put on *Where the Places Meet.* It's almost time to reveal and complete it.

But that damned dead bug is still stuck between the panes.

Then I know what to do. I prop one of my try-out paintings on the window sill to hide all signs of the dead creature. A study of me, Rachel and my companion: the young woman pressed between two lovers as they pass from human form. *Trio.* I'd painted it quickly. The speed shows in the splashes of colour and the motion of transformation and attraction.

Trio looks just right with a view of the city behind it, lit up at night. All the things I paint are present in our city centres, though they may be hidden.

Now the lift is coming up with the first guests. More people are bounding up the stairs as if they're too impatient to wait for the lift. Voices echo between the floors. No one seems to care about being fashionably late.

Leading the first arrivals is a square-jawed but slightly built man in an expensive-looking jacket. He's clean-cut to the point of blandness, except for the light in his eyes as he throws open his arms and nearly knocks a tree over with his briefcase.

"Rory! I haven't seen you in ages, man. Someone told me you had something on!"

Rory looks confused, then there's an answering light in his eyes. "*Smelly!* What the fuck!"

"I'm called Sam now, but *you're* allowed to call me Smelly. Just tonight, mind."

"Wanna drink, Smelly?"

"Nah, I'm strictly straight-edge these days. I brought my own pomegranate juice and all." He opens his briefcase and produces a red bottle.

As the people crowd in, I listen. This time the laughter is turned up a notch, yet punctuated by more silence. Some people just look. They are waiting. Others nod at each other in recognition.

"This juice is intense stuff. Organic and all . . . Go on, have a sip." Smelly is still urging Rory to abandon his lager. "Hey, if you ever need a website, I'm your man!"

There's that woman with the long white plait again, looking with expectation at the trees and overhanging ivy. She cocks her head as if she waits to hear something too.

So I put on the old pipe-music cassette. I adjust the lighting so it deepens the shadows in the paintings. With the heat generated by people now crowding into the room, I'm already eager to lie in their coolness.

"Helen, you look fabulous!" Nao gushes as she enters the room, tugging at my silk semi-sheer mulberry-coloured gown.

I shrug. "It's just an old thing I pulled from the cupboard. Come, sit down."

I settle into the padding of one of Rory's twisted car-seats. I point to its companion piece under a leather-bound tree.

Nao stands back. "Uhm, is that for sitting in?" She looks at the cupped hand of metal as if it's likely to close around her and remove her from the world.

"What do you think I'm doing?" I laugh. "It's really comfortable. You should try it."

Nao levers her pert little bottom into the chair. It swallows her up. I only see her legs sticking out of its cup of metal at awkward angles.

"Help," she is squeaking. "I can't get up!" Sudden fear inflames her voice.

"Just relax," I advise her. "Chill out. These comfy chairs are part of the exhibition."

"They might be interesting to look at, but art and furniture are two different things. And I'm allergic to these plants. Get me out of this!"

I rise and I'm about to extend my hand to her. But someone gets there first.

"Hey, you alright? Need help?" It's Jonny, reaching in.

"Yes, please!" Nao stretches out to clasp Jonny's hand. She is hauled up and set on her feet. Immediately, she assumes a military bearing as she brushes off her clothes.

"You alright?" Jonny asks again. "I'll get you a drink."

"Thanks. White wine will do." She examines the chair again. "These chairs *are* interesting. And those trees! Who made them?"

"Rory. The guy you called a loser. I can give you his number." I look in my purse for his card, but I only have the one for removals. My little brother still hasn't made up new ones.

131

Jonny appears with Nao's wine and a lager for himself. "This'll help you recover from your ordeal in Rory's chair. Some of the stuff here can be . . . intimidating."

"Speaking of which, I'm surprised to see *you* here," I tell him.

"It's Rory's big night, innit? I can't miss that, though he told me he wouldn't be offended if I stayed away. But I've had counselling, and we talked again about facing my fears. So that's what I'm doing. Facing them. *Embracing* them." He spreads his arms out in an expansive gesture. "Not to mention keeping an eye out for attractive art students."

"Now that's the spirit, Jonny. I wish you luck with the latter. I'll keep a look out myself. Hey, a nice girl called Hopi has just arrived, a regular visitor. I've already had one success as a matchmaker with Rory and Mandy, so I'll go over and have a word."

Hopi has already settled in front of *Trio*. She sits in a chair with her legs crossed like a kid waiting for a story in a crèche, but there's a most unchildlike gleam to her gaze. Another woman joins Hopi, leaning against a leather tree. She has a familiar face—long, oval with deep brown eyes and a solemn Renaissance gaze. But there's nothing ethereal about her voluptuous build, barely contained within her T-shirt and denim mini.

I realise it's Franklin Forbes' daughter. I go to greet her. I never did get around to replying to her father's email but that obviously hasn't put her off.

"Helen," she exclaims before I say anything. "I *must* speak to you. My name's Natasha. They've been trying to keep me away from you. They sent me somewhere to 'rest', but it's really a posh prison. I'm meant to have lessons, but they're shit and I've escaped!" Her hands punctuate her words as they stroke the skin of Rory's tree trunk next to her.

"Well done!" I put my arm around her and whisper in her ear. "I know what it's like. My stepfather hated me and sent me to boarding schools. They try to make you just like every other empty-headed *lady*. But you have *something* inside you. You must nurture it; water it like a plant. And it'll grow into this . . . " I gesture around the room. "Or something better."

Natasha nods. "Yes, yes, exactly! And it's not only me. I wanted to bring friends. Other people in this place have seen your paintings. They don't allow us to keep our own photos. We don't have the internet or anything. But we remember what we've seen, and talk about it with each other."

I pat Natasha on the shoulder. "I'm so glad you can make it. The painting we'll be working on is still covered. But I'm just about to get it ready . . . "

When I go to do just that, I see Natasha is now sitting next to Hopi and talking. I'm not sure whether she is talking to Hopi, or to the painting.

When I unveil *Where the Places Meet*, everyone stops their conversation, and they gather in front of it. A few people stand near the Roman pillar, gazing at its markings. Smelly traces them with his finger, then moves his head back and forth as if trying to follow a tennis game. The white-haired woman gazes at the pillar too.

Others stand back to see more of the painting. I deliberately didn't look at it for a few days, so now I see it as new. Here's the pillar, the hillside, the field. There's me, Rachel and my companion entwined and moving in the grass, other companions twisting and turning around each other.

There's the tunnel of trees at the end of Rachel's field, the green hole.

There are many vanishing points: at the end of the tunnel, the scattered baby teeth that turn to stars, to black holes.

And at the centre of the grove stands a presence in the green, waiting to be seen.

"The . . ." Johnny's pointing, looking as if he's facing an onrushing train.

"Don't *you* start." I cover Jonny's mouth with my hand.

Jonny is trembling, but I hear a muffled "It's OK . . ." from under my hand. I allow him to prise it away.

"It's OK, Helen," he says, "I was only going to say 'the painting is awesome'."

"Sorry if I had a go, Jonny. Maybe I'm just a bit stressed. But are you sure you don't want to sit down or go out for some fresh air? I imagine you're still feeling fragile."

"Don't worry. I can cope."

"I'll make sure he behaves himself," says Nao, smiling at Jonny. "Say, Mr . . ."

"Jonny."

"Yes, Jonny. I hear you've had a very extreme reaction to Ms Vaughan's work. Could you tell me about it?"

"Doesn't everyone? Don't *you*, or do you try to hide it and be cool? I've seen . . ."

"Jonny, dealing with odd or discomfiting work is an occupational hazard. So let's sit down by the window and have a chat." Nao takes Jonny by the arm and leads him away.

Mandy also stands in front of the window, rather strained and red-faced as she fans herself with a handful of publicity leaflets. Rory has a reassuring arm around her.

I know what's bothering her. The cassette has finished. I go to rewind it and watch as my companion's music slips into peoples' minds again. I see it in the distracted way they listen to each other as they strain to hear something else. I turn it up louder.

There's a rhythm in the way people walk to and fro, closer, backward and forward again. I move among them, handing out brushes. I point to pots of paints laid out on the tables. There are other substances too. Oils and unguents; ordinary linseed and others that smell of roses, almonds, pepper and musk. Locks of fur and hair I've collected over the years, mementos of many transformations: they're curly, woolly, straight and silky. Ice blonde and coal black; auburn and ginger. There's an inlaid stone pot holding puffs of down.

I go to that unfinished portrait of my younger self, my mother at my shoulder. On me her eyes are redrawn as almond-shaped, the skin is olive and the full lips fuller. Every feature so similar, yet exaggerated in a way that turns beauty to repulsion and back to beauty again.

I look my painted Helen in the eye. Dr Raymond once said I had no soul. But what do I see here? There is desire, which is good enough.

I kiss myself on the lips. Yes, I am ready to start.

I spread both arms, and lay down broad strokes around the painted Helen. Then I move my focus beyond her . . . to Rachel, to the path she takes across that field. I lay down hints of my companion next to her.

I've painted him many times. But each is different. Now he is looking beyond the boundaries of the painting. He is also in the grove, parting the branches, parting the mist.

I paint with my hips thrust forward. My brush describes curves; it travels down angles and planes. My strokes find a rhythm. *Swish, swish*. Back and forth, back and forth.

I look over my shoulder. Everyone now stays a respectful distance away. Too respectful.

"Come on," I urge. "Don't be shy. Turn the music up, Mandy!"

So the pipe music grows louder until it's a drill in the forehead, letting you see what wasn't seen before. I think of the sway of Rachel's hips under my hands as we went to meet my companion. And here everyone shifts back and forth on their feet in the same rhythm. Scents of sweat and perfume waft through the room.

At last, someone breaks rank and moves forward. Natasha.

As she comes close to the painting the room is so quiet I can hear the touch of her breasts against the canvas. Her hands open and close at its surface like hungry mouths as she arches her back.

A tall man with long dark curls walks up behind her and eases her skirt up and her knickers down. The man turns. It's *him*. There's a shock as our eyes meet. Just as I'm about to speak, he beckons. *Come.* He steps into the glade on the canvas.

He was *here* . . . and now he's *there*.

Natasha is left, leaning. She shows no sign of noticing or caring how she is exposed. Though the room is filled with people and they all watch her, she stands alone pressed against that painting, her hands grappling at it with a sound that reminds me of that bug batting against the glass.

Someone has to help her get in there. But no one has the guts to do it yet.

I dip my broadest sable brush into the most fragrant, richest oil. Then I go to her and swish it down between her buttocks, then forward, back and forth between her legs. I am gentle. I take my time. She is moaning softly, swaying against the canvas and back onto my brush. Scents rise from the warmed oil, scents of flowers and the forest, roasted nutmeg. I breathe them in and they fill me.

The tape has finished. There is no other sound for a while.

Then there are stirrings throughout the room, soft and voiceless at first. They grow into murmurs and sighs, into another kind of song. I've heard it many times, but each time I hear it as new. The song strokes my neck; its lower register vibrates at my core.

I hum it, my lips to Natasha's ear. I press another brush into her hand, a delicate one capable of the barest wisps of colour and form. "See the man in the woods with the pipes? Draw the music coming out of them, and he will play for us. Paint now and our pleasure will continue. If we keep painting we'll find a way in."

With a gasp she adds threads of colour in front of her. I make my own strokes with the sable brush. I use a sponge with my other hand, squeezing and pressing it between her plump thighs. The colour she lays down finds the right places. It tints the sound of pleasuring behind us, makes it rise.

And I hear echoes, faraway sounds from unknown throats. Some are shrill, others deep. The pipes weave around the swelling chorus.

Each swing of a brush adds another cascade of notes, joined by sighs from Natasha. I draw her closer as she quivers. The eager voices grow into a wave that pushes us, pulls us forward. She flings out an arm in front of her, fingers extended. When I put my hand over hers, the tips of my fingers are met by something denser than air, but lighter than water.

Natasha moves through it, exclaiming at its touch. I watch wonder fill her face and I hold her tighter. "Keep dancing, keep touching, it will keep away any fear," I urge. I apply my broad brush to her with more strength, quickening the rhythm. Air flows over us and pulls close. It is smooth, slick, more fragrant than rose oil. We slip between panes that reflect the palest green, cool violet, lime and mint. Fine points of light burst over our skin. Natasha twists in my arms, squeezing her legs tight around my brush. Her drawn-out shout vibrates against me, through me. The air strokes my skin in the same rhythm.

The trees reach for each other over my head, branches clasping, parting and entangling. Leaves of the glade unfurl and spread their fingers, stroke us with insistence as we travel down the tunnel of trees.

We're in the forest where the trees have supple skin for bark and the waters reach for us. I've been here before. But this time each colour and shadow is bolder than anything I've ever painted. Every colour contains millions of others. Nothing is flat. I see the wind, a hint of blue that changes to lemon when I blink, then to every other colour, a constant prism, like the shift on the horizon when my companion parted the branches of the grove. They sound a chord of resonance that welcomes me home.

Between the trees I glimpse hills and fields I haven't drawn yet. A large bird coasts on the air, spreading blood-red wings. There are cliffs like teeth in an open mouth letting loose a discordant song.

And my companion joins the song with his pipes, standing in front of me. He plays seven pipes for seven notes, strains that hold the matter of the world together. Now he is fair-haired, his eyes green as the glade he stands in. He whirls with his music and with each whirl he changes. His skin is dark, he grows pale again. He is a man, then a woman. He grows wings and he loses them, he clicks hooves upon the stones. He can be anything, everything. So can I, soon.

We whirl together. He enfolds me in warmth, he thrusts in me and then I turn and take him. My hair grows into black vines that taste the changing texture of his skin. I wrap around him. We are life. We are matter, ever-changing and ever-flowing.

Then Natasha slips between us. I surround and stroke her too. "Look at him, look at us," I say to her. "This is what you've been seeking. Are you glad you found it?"

Natasha's eyes are unfocused but avid. Her lips first form a word that may be "yes". She sways and turns within my ivy, touches me under the tattered silk of my gown. "More, Helen . . . More people are coming with us. They can't put us all away, can they?"

For others have followed into the breach, led by Rory's friend Smelly and the white-haired woman. Some show confusion as it becomes clear they're no longer in Shoreditch. But formerly fearful Jonny now rolls and laughs in the grass with his new love— Nao.

Wind sprites whirl others about in warm gusts, persuasive, as clothes are shed. The "Defend Shoreditch?" T-shirt drifts to the ground near our feet. There's Ben, the dancer Hopi met at the last showing. A knot of people caress each other around a tree, while the pink-haired guy from the Belfry clutches the tree and moves into its recess.

Others join the movements on the ground. Flashes of gleaming skin, light and dark, half-hidden by long grass. There is thrashing and shaking in the undergrowth, long moans. Laughter rises in gulps and gasps on the edge of a scream.

Natasha is kissing me on the neck, her breath is fast again. Her lips are soft, *his* hands even softer. The wind that touches everyone touches me too and carries their excitement with it.

"Let's go over there now," Natasha whispers in my ear. "Let's join them in the grass."

"Helen?" Hopi is tugging at me. "Where are we? Where . . . Why is the ground crawling? And why do the trees have skin and the leaves are hands? *Why are the rocks singing?*" Her voice is tremulous, her cheeks flushed as if someone had just slapped her on each one. Two tufts of hair stick up as if she's become a little Panisca.

"But look what I found," Hopi's voice switches into a brighter register. "Isn't this cool? I can use it in my next installation." She holds a fist-sized flower shaped like a star, with a deep brown eye in the middle that slowly blinks. The creases in the petals around it look like lines left by a smile. I can see why Hopi is fond of it.

Then Hopi frowns. "Helen, you look . . . different. You okay?"

"I'm fine, Hopi." I touch her lightly and a convulsive sigh moves through her. My companion kisses her, lifts her up and up and up. She floats on the wind, her mouth a hole of surprise. Then laughter.

"Dance!" he orders. "Then you won't fall down unless you want to."

Ben receives Hopi when she returns to earth. If the colours of this world have a beat, he finds it in his steps as he whirls her down the path behind my companion.

But where are Rory and Mandy?

"Let's go," my companion urges. "Dance and we'll get there."

People are now up and clutching each other in a shambling conga line. Their movements are fluid, their limbs stretched in the shimmering air. Bruises and red marks appear where they grip and pinch too hard, taking on shapes like the marks I made on the Roman column. The white-haired woman displays those marks in black and green on her arms and her inner thigh as she steps forward.

My companion changes the tune and I hear strains of "The Two Magicians". They stir memories of Rachel, of my duet with Mandy. But he sings yet another version. Many more than two magicians enter the dance, and it's not so clear who changes into what. The tempo breaks into a wayward spiral of a jig as we come out of the forest and up a hill. A distant city to the right emits clouds of smoke, its shape dark and alluring.

"Are we going there?" I nod towards the city.

"No, no . . ." says my companion. "I'm going further than that. I'm going past the vanishing point, *all* of them." He gestures ahead, past the top of the hill, into a grove, at the city. "You and your paintings have helped me. It's in the balance of things to each other, the intensity of desire, in resonance. Now I can go home!"

I grip his hand tighter. "You said I couldn't come with you, but I was very young. I made a life in the place we've just left, but now I know I can't go back there. The colours are too pale . . . " A crash and commotion interrupts me.

"*Helen!* Where the fuck are we?"

There are scratches down Rory's arms from stumbling in underbrush. He's lost his glasses, but he sees enough to recognise my companion. He points an accusing finger at him. "It's you, you fucking freak! You've got a lot of explaining to do, *Dad!*"

My companion wraps him in a full embrace. "There you are, son. You've grown up well. Better than some of the others." He kisses Rory now, and as the kiss lingers he begins to change. He grows again into the tall young man with dark curls, his fingers fine and long as they stroke Rory's hair from his face and linger on his cheek.

Rory pushes him away. "Get off me. And don't think you'll fool me by growing a pair of tits either, you stinking old pervert."

"You liked my tits well enough when I was your mother. Such a hungry baby . . . "

"You're worse than a stinking old pervert, you're . . . "

"Rory, there's no need to be so rude . . . " I start. But my companion touches my hand and points, urging me to follow on the path he has chosen. On either side the grass is tall and whispering, and he whispers back to it as he starts to stroll down the path.

I look back at Rory. "Come on," I urge. Then I look ahead to my companion setting out through the grass. And back at Rory.

I'll miss him. Realising that I'll miss Rory hits me as hard as the colours of this world. Rory is more like me than my companion. He's been a companion too, even we clashed.

I wave again at Rory to come along.

"Helen, stop for a moment."

"Hurry up, Rory. We'll be left behind."

"Who says I want to go? Why are you following *him*? He's shit! He only abandoned you later than he abandoned me."

"It's not like that!"

"So what's it like, Hel? Besides, I'm not going anywhere without Mandy. She was looking for her accordion. And she's not here."

"Mandy will be fine. Come on."

Rory tugs at my arm, shouting. "And what've you done leading these people here? They'll go mad once they stop partying and see where they are . . . "

"They *wanted* to come. Most of them are misfits who need to go somewhere else. Like us. And have you had a look? They won't be the same. Nothing will be the same."

More people collect around us. Some are holding their clothing, others are still naked. They're rubbing their eyes, looking at each other. They don't seem sure whether to watch the fight, or go back to shagging and dancing.

Smelly wanders off to put his arm down a flower the size of a bin lid, with meaty petals layered in ivory and pale yellow. He moves his arm down further, up and down, opening his own mouth to breathe in its sharp-scented pollen.

Hopi is hanging on to her own flower. "It's died," she tells me in a trembling voice.

"Helen, are you listening to me?"

The white-haired woman embraces Smelly from behind, wrapping her arms around him, reaching down. He opens his mouth wide enough to swallow all the light around us, keening in his ecstasy. Then he yelps, trying to jerk his arm out of the flower's moving calyx. "Get me out of here!" He pulls harder. "Let go, you blossoming bastard!"

Nao crouches nearby, taking pictures on her BlackBerry.

"For fuck's sake, Smelly. Get a grip." Rory runs over to give the flower a kick that leaves a pulpy hole at its heart.

It springs open and Smelly draws out his arm, flexing slimy fingers. "Thanks, mate . . . "

"Don't thank me. Just get the hell back home to your pomegranate juice and web pages and Facebook and whatever . . . All of you!" He turns to the rest of our party. "Hey guys, we're going home. It's too weird here. We have *lives* to go to. Let that fucker with the pipes fuck off and let's go home."

"Speak for yourself. I'm not going back. I'm staying with Helen!" Natasha declares. "Why should I go back there and get put away again? Not when there's this world in front of us. It's, like, wonderful. It takes me out of myself. I'm free here. It's full of great sex."

"You've only seen a little bit. You have no idea what it's really like," Rory argues.

Nao is still snapping photos, one after another. Her lips are pressed together, her eyes large in an intent, elongated face. Perhaps Nao takes those pictures so *she* won't fall down.

"I won't be staying here," she says. "I have an article to finish, *and* a new boyfriend."

She squeezes Jonny's hand and grins. "So once I make notes and take my photos we're going back. I made sure I knew the way back in case my GPS doesn't work. I remember that much from Girl Guides."

Jonny hesitates, then withdraws his hand from Nao's. "Nah, I don't wanna go back to that shithole. It's alright for you with your criticising and your fancy stuff."

Jonny is the calmest I've seen him. Perhaps some of this is familiar territory.

"But what do you like here, Jonny?" Rory asks. "The important thing is that we've shared it and we'll be changed by our experience. It doesn't have to be the same shithole when we go back. Once people find out that *this* exists . . . "

"Find out about what, this world you mean? Yeah, all the rich fuckers at home will snatch up the real estate here and turn it into a theme park. It's better if they don't find out."

"Of course they'll find out because I'm going to tell them," says Nao. "This will be the story of the century and it's *mine*."

"Is that all you think about?" barks Rory. "Your fucking career and being famous?"

Arguments explode among the group and that flat "morning-after" feeling seeps everywhere. I should be angry at Rory for ruining the party, for stopping the dance. But at least we got here. If I had any doubts about leaving my old life behind, listening to this lot has blown them away.

Hopi sits on the ground apart from the rest with her head down between her knees, which she hugs tightly. Yes, she should return before it's too late. And that boy who's crying with his face down in the grass. Nao can bring them back and sit them down for an interview. Someone else will put on the kettle.

But I must try to make Rory see sense, just one more time. I lightly lay a hand on his shoulder, knowing how nervous he is about me touching him. The kinship between us is still there, warming the tips of my fingers. I know he feels it too.

"Listen to me, Rory. After what you've learned, do you think you can go back to your old life as a driver and art dabbler who gets treated with contempt? Do you think you can live a normal life? You know how different you are from people back there. Won't you be lonely?"

Rory turns to me. He's thoughtful now. "Maybe. But my mates will still be my mates."

"No, it's not like that. You'll be wondering how they can be your mates if they don't know the most important thing about you. Mandy doesn't know, does she?"

He nods. Maybe I'm getting through to him.

144

"But I can't leave Mandy," he says. "Not when we've just found each other. And I promised to take the kid—you know, my ex's son—to a computer fair next week!"

He pauses, then bursts out with even more passion. "And what about my flat? I can't leave behind a council flat in Highgate with a garden! People would *kill* to have that!"

That's it. I give up. "Fuck you and your flat. I'm tempted to kill you for such stupidity, but I'm in a hurry. I'm going."

For my companion, the one that some call the Great God Pan, is getting further and further away, receding into the fields and the hazy horizon.

I walk faster and then run, trying to keep him in my sight.

When I glance back for a moment, Rory is still bellowing and waving his arms at the others. They aren't dancing now.

It is much later when I stop walking. I've passed over the crest of the hill, and in front of me there's another hill, a river and the dark fringe of more forest. I can no longer see my companion. The shifting ground shows no sign of his tracks. It's no use trying to follow.. For a moment I hear that bug batting and buzzing within the double-glazing, struggling until it died. *The panes will grind you.*

But it's not like that here, is it? The sky is high above me. The fields and forests and the city streets should be bountiful. I'm not alone. Sprites call from the rivers and ponds. The wind is blowing through the long grass and I hear its whispers. Other sprites form in the wind and stroke me with cool fingers. The stones sing their challenge, and I answer with a song of my own. The dark city beckons with a bass rumble of concrete and roads and hidden parks.

Did Rachel die over a hundred years ago? Or does she still roam through that city, or move across these fields or these skies?

145

Will I even recognise her if she does?

Nothing is certain here, and that's why I belong.

And I still know the path back to London and to Wales and Argentina and beyond. If I can't go forward with my companion, I'll travel through the dreams of my old world—just as he once did. I don't have his pipes but I have my voice. I'll sing and paint pictures on the walls of their cities, splash them with the colours I discover in this world. I'll show them what lies beyond the things in front of them, and get them to dance and fuck and sing and light my way to the space between the places, home to the point where all places meet.